MORE ADVENTURES IN THE ARIA & LIAM BOOK SERIES

The Coded Papyrus

Enigma in Rome

The Cursed Empress

The Sun Disk

The Magic Chalice

The Great Christmas Rescue

The Druids' Secret

The Baker Street Mystery

The Sun King (2026)

APICEM PUBLISHING

Apicem Publishing
1309 Coffeen Avenue STE 1200
Sheridan, WY 82801, United States
www.apicempublishing.com

This paperback edition 2025
3

ISBN (paperback): 978-1-959814-26-9
ISBN (ebook): 978-1-959814-17-7

For information regarding permission, please write to Apicem Publishing: tellus@apicempublishing.com.

Our books may be purchased in bulk for promotional, educational, or business use. Please contact your local bookseller or Apicem Publishing by email at tellus@apicempublishing.com.

COLINE MONSARRAT

presents

ARIA & LIAM
AND THE ENIGMA IN ROME

APICEM PUBLISHING

HEY FELLOW ADVENTURERS! MEET LIAM, MY BEST FRIEND AND PARTNER IN CRIME.

HE'S A THIRTEEN-YEAR-OLD KID FROM SOMMETVILLE WHO CAN CODE LIKE A WIZARD, KICK A SOCCER BALL LIKE A PRO, AND PLAY THE PIANO SO WELL BEETHOVEN WOULD BE SPEECHLESS. (BUT SERIOUSLY, DON'T TELL HIM I SAID THAT. HIS HEAD'S BIG ENOUGH ALREADY!) WHEN LIAM'S NOT BUSY ACING SCHOOL, YOU CAN USUALLY FIND HIM DOING ONE OF THOSE THINGS.

UNLESS, OF COURSE, I'VE GOT SOME WILD IDEA TO DRAG US INTO TROUBLE. AND LET'S BE HONEST, I USUALLY DO! LIKE THE TIME I ACCIDENTALLY CRACKED OPEN A PORTAL TO THE PAST AND LAUNCHED US INTO OUR FIRST ADVENTURE. (LIAM'S STILL DEBATING WHETHER TO THANK ME OR THROTTLE ME FOR THAT ONE!)

SURE, MY HISTORICAL KNOW-HOW HAS SAVED OUR BUTTS A FEW TIMES, BUT CREDIT WHERE CREDIT'S DUE: LIAM'S MAD ARCHERY SKILLS HAVE BEEN TOTAL LIFESAVERS. WITHOUT HIM, WE'D PROBABLY STILL BE STUCK IN SOME MEDIEVAL DUNGEON!

NOW, WE'RE BASICALLY TIME-TRAVELING HEROES, SAVING CIVILIZATIONS AND MAKING SURE HISTORY STAYS ON TRACK. AND WHILE LIAM ALWAYS PRETENDS TO FREAK OUT WHEN WE LAND IN ANOTHER TIME PERIOD, I KNOW HE SECRETLY LOVES IT.

HEY THERE, FELLOW ADVENTURERS! LET ME INTRODUCE YOU TO MY BEST FRIEND, ARIA.

SHE'S NOT YOUR AVERAGE THIRTEEN-YEAR-OLD. THIS GIRL IS OBSESSED WITH HISTORY. SERIOUSLY, DON'T EVEN THINK ABOUT CHALLENGING HER TO A HISTORY QUIZ, SHE'LL BEAT YOU EVERY SINGLE TIME. THAT'S WHY I CALL HER THE WALKING ENCYCLOPEDIA.
ARIA'S ALL ABOUT LIVING LIFE TO THE FULLEST, EVEN IF IT MEANS BREAKING A FEW RULES

(WHICH SEEMS TO HAPPEN A LOT WHEN I'M AROUND, FOR SOME REASON). BUT HONESTLY, IT'S HER CURIOSITY THAT GOT US INTO THIS WHOLE TIME-TRAVELING ADVENTURE IN THE FIRST PLACE. WE ENDED UP IN THE KINGDOM OF RAMESSES II, A PLACE SO OLD IT MAKES MY GRANDPA'S GRANDPA'S GRANDPA LOOK YOUNG.

When we were young, she started calling me "my dear Liam," saying it made us sound like we lived in some grandiose era of the past (her words, not mine!). I thought it was hilarious, so I followed suit and started calling her "my dear Aria." Little did I know it would turn out to be a premonition of our time-traveling escapades!

At first, I wasn't exactly thrilled about being dragged into the past whenever someone needed our help. But I'll admit it's kind of grown on me. Just, you know, don't tell Aria I said that. She'll never let me live it down.

Of course, we can't introduce each other without mentioning our furry best friend, Pingo. We adopted him after our adventure in Atlantis, and now he's part of the team. When we're not all together (which almost never happens!), Pingo bounces between our two houses.

Oh, and did I mention that Aria and I live just a few houses apart? Talk about a best friend dream come true!

THE CHARACTERS

ARIA

LIAM

TIRO

MARCIA

GAIA

TITUS

AELLO

SEPTIMUS

OLIVERUS

CAIUS

MOGURIX

MAP OF THE ROMAN EMPIRE

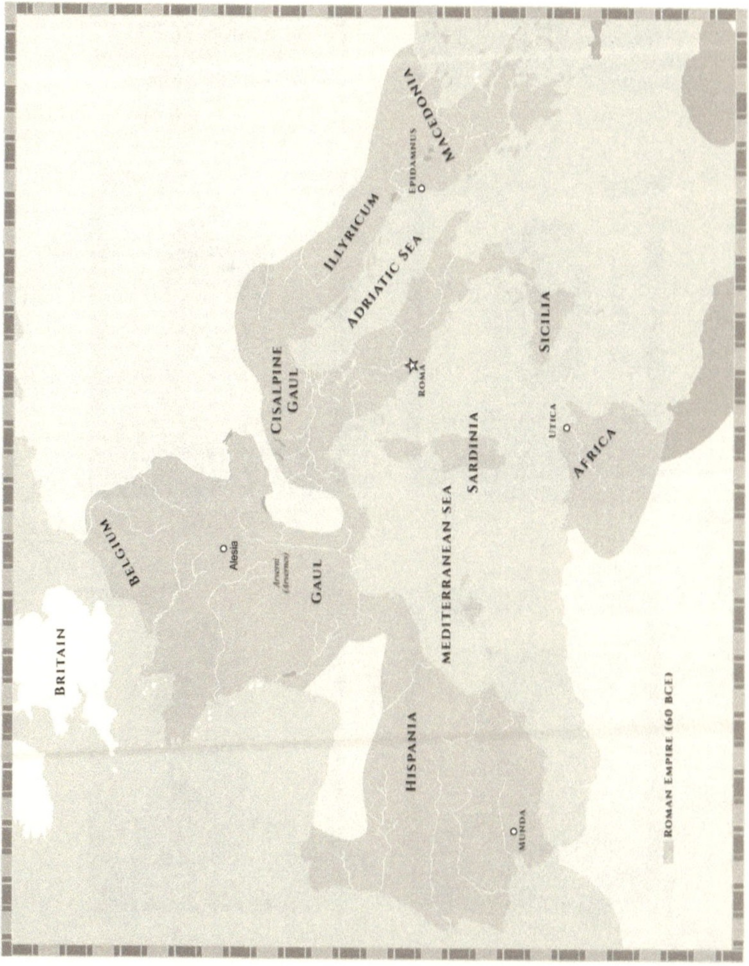

ONE
THE BULLIED

Liam steps off Sommetville Junior High School's outdoor basketball court to take a short break. A chilly breeze brushes past him, sending goosebumps up his arms. He shivers and pulls at the sleeves of his T-shirt, wishing he'd worn something warmer. It's not even winter yet, and he's already dreading the layers of clothes, stiff jackets, and itchy scarves. He hates feeling trapped under them all.

At the center of the court, his best friend Aria shifts from foot to foot with the ball held tightly between her hands a few inches from her waist, as if it were a stink bomb ready to explode.

Liam watches her and laughs. "Aria! You know the ball's not going to attack you, right?"

"What do you mean? I'm totally ready to shoot. Don't break my concentration."

"Okay, okay … just saying."

"Do you think you're the only one who can make free throws? Just watch this."

Liam forms circles with his thumbs and index fingers and holds them up like glasses. "My eyes are wide open."

Aria moves forward and stops a few feet away from the hoop just before the white free-throw line. She tosses the ball from hand to hand.

Despite not making a single basket since the class began weeks ago, she refuses to give up. She shakes off her doubts, bends her knees, and jumps as she throws the ball. It misses the backboard and bounces off the court, taking Aria's hope with it. The ball lands between three of their classmates. Amelia scoops it up and throws it back to Liam.

"You need to fix the angle of your arm," Liam says to Aria. "You're throwing too far to the left. That's why your shots are off. Watch me," he says, lining up a shot.

In seconds, the ball goes through the net—no big deal. He tosses it back to Aria, who catches it like it's heavier than a bowling ball. Her arms sink, and her back bends. She mutters a quiet, "Thanks," and gets back into position. Once again, the ball ignores her intention and bounces across the court, rolling to a stop in the grass at the court's edge.

Her frustration builds. She hates it when she can't do something well.

"You'll get better. It takes time to improve at a sport," Liam says. "You can't expect to be great at everything right away."

"I don't expect—"

Aria's cut off by a familiar, unwelcome voice. "So, Miss I-Know-Everything can't shoot a ball," their classmate Oliver yells from the other end of the court, laughing in a smug, fake way that Aria and Liam hate.

"I'd love to see you try," Liam fires back. "I doubt you'd do any better than Aria."

Oliver sneers at Aria, who clenches her fists so hard her knuckles crack. "You can't even defend yourself?" He laughs louder.

"I don't need anyone to defend me," Aria says. "And coming from a guy who can't come to school without his mom holding his hand, your wisecracks are pretty ironic. Back off, or else…"

"Or else what? Gonna call your mommy?" Oliver says, eyes glinting. "Oh wait … she's dead!"

Liam's jaw tightens. "You went too far, Oliver. Take that back. Now."

Aria's face turns the same shade of red as her Sommetville gym-class tee. She opens her mouth, but no words come. Tears well up in her eyes, which only makes her angrier.

Oliver grins and pulls something from behind his back. "You better be nice to me, or I'll destroy your precious notebook."

It takes Aria a few seconds to realize what she's seeing. The gold dress of Cleopatra on the cover of her blue journal shimmers as Oliver waves it around. She carries the notebook everywhere, scribbling down every idea or thought that pops into her head.

"Did you go through my bag?" she blurts out. "How dare you! Give it back!" Aria lunges, but Oliver lifts the notebook high, just out of reach.

Her eyes are spilling over now, and it fuels Oliver's mocking laugh. "What? Are you crying? You are such a little girl!"

"Oliver, stop!" Liam shouts. He picks up his pace as

he crosses the court and reaches for the notebook in Oliver's hands.

Before he can grab it, Aria pushes Oliver from the side. He stumbles back, and the book slips from his hand.

But Aria doesn't pick it up. Instead, she bolts off the court toward the school building, biting her lip to keep any more angry tears from spilling. The rage inside her grows, a small flame turning into a roaring fire until it consumes every part of her.

Liam glares at the other boy. "You're such a jerk, Oliver. That's why no one wants to hang out with you." Without a backward glance, he takes off after Aria.

"Aw, go chase your girlfriend, Liam!" Oliver says while rubbing the spot on his arm where Aria pushed him.

Liam ignores him and runs faster. "Aria! Wait for me!"

"I just want to be alone," she calls over her shoulder, wiping her face with her sleeve.

"Don't let him get to you. He does it to everyone. He's just mean."

"I know," Aria says, her voice tight. "But I need to be alone right now."

With both hands, she pushes through the swinging

doors leading to the west wing of the school. The doors slam against the walls and bounce back right at Liam's face. He catches them just in time.

As Liam opens the doors, he says, "I get it. But I want you to know I'm here if you need anything." He steps inside but freezes as a bird swoops straight at him. He ducks, barely avoiding a collision, and it flutters away into the sky. Liam straightens, his expression mirroring the shock on Aria's face.

He's not standing in the school hallway as he should be. The posters for the school's upcoming Christmas show are gone. So is the wooden flooring that runs halfway up the walls, topped by off-white paint that reaches the ceiling.

Aria and Liam stand on uneven stone pavement. Dead grass sprouts from cracks along the path. Aria looks down and lifts her foot from a square stone carved with the letters *SPQR*. Senatus Populusque Romanus, she recalls from Latin class.

A foul smell hits them without warning. Liam winces and covers his nose, but his eyes stay fixed on the street ahead. Houses line both sides, their beige, dirt-stained walls standing out against red-brick roofs. The sun is shining, yet even with its warmth, Liam feels a chill.

He spins around to open the doors behind him, but they're gone too.

He swallows hard and turns to Aria, who stares ahead like she just landed on an alien planet. He waves a hand in front of her face. Nothing. She doesn't even blink.

His breathing quickens. His chest tightens. Where are they?

A young girl and a tiny white dog burst from around the corner of the building nearest to them, racing in their direction.

Her pastel-pink dress, long and flowy, is streaked with brown at the hem where it brushes the ground. Curly blonde hair frames her oval face, and a pink head-band sets off the blush on her cheeks. Her blue eyes almost disappear beneath the fear on her face.

The clang of metal pulls their attention from the girl to two men running toward them. Metal wrist guards clash against their body armor as they charge with swords raised high.

"Run! They're going to kill us!" the girl screams at Aria and Liam, who are standing in the middle of the street.

Snapping back to life, Aria grabs Liam's arm. "Come on!"

TWO
ROME

A woman steps out of her home with a basket in her arms. As Aria runs closer, she sees her bend to pick up a few pieces of wood piled near the door. The woman's head snaps up at the sound of their running footsteps. She gasps, drops the wood, and darts back inside, slamming the door just as the girl and her dog race past with Aria and Liam close behind.

The girl turns left into an alley barely wide enough for two people to run side by side. Tall jars and bundles of hay stand in rows in front of the houses, making the path even tighter.

Aria's knee buckle, and she stumbles, but braces against a wall before she goes down. She pushes forward and runs fast enough to catch up with Liam.

Behind them, footsteps pound and armor clanks, growing louder.

"They're getting closer. We have to go faster," Liam says.

The girl veers right and darts down another passage so narrow that almost no sunlight reaches them. After a few strides, they reach a street buzzing with life.

"We need to slow down, or people will notice something's wrong," the girl says to Aria and Liam. Her voice isn't quite a child's, but not yet a woman's either. "Follow me."

They enter the street and weave through the crowd. Some people are walking through the throng, while others stand around, as if trying to block the way. The little white dog, barely as tall as three apples stacked one atop the other, leads the way. It manages to soar over a puddle without slowing down.

Liam glances back but sees no sign of the two armed men who were chasing them. Hopefully, they've lost their pursuers.

"Ouch," he mutters as his waist bumps a table, sending a melon rolling to the ground. He rubs his side and looks ahead. On both sides of the street, the houses are barely visible behind all the people selling their goods. Tables filled with vegetables and fruit are squeezed in beside stalls loaded high with meat. Men and women with baskets tucked in the crooks of their elbows jostle each other as if battling for the best items.

It looks like an ancient version of the Sommetville farmer's market, the one Aria and Liam visit every Saturday morning.

A group of children runs right between Aria and Liam as they laugh and chase one another, caught up in their game.

Liam tugs his T-shirt away from his chest. Sweat soaks the fabric, making it feel three times heavier. Maybe it's the running that's made him so hot, or maybe fear is tightening its grip on him. He glances at the people around him, how they dress and speak, and there's no doubt in his mind—unless this is some kind of huge costume festival that the junior high is putting on, he and Aria have traveled through time again.

The dog races down a side street, and the girl hurries after it. She stops beside a haystack, crouches, and signals for Aria and Liam to do the same. They duck just as a man's shout echoes from the alley's opening.

Peering cautiously around the pile of hay, Liam spots the two armed men staring directly at the haystack. He pulls back and covers his mouth with his hand to quiet his panting.

A few silent seconds pass. He looks again.

They're gone.

Liam's shoulders drop, and he lets out a sigh, leaning back against the wall behind them.

"What's going on? Where are we?" he asks the girl.

But Aria answers first. "The carving on the stone, *SPQR*. The Senate and People of Rome. We're in Rome, Liam. And based on how people are dressed, I'm guessing we traveled back around 2100 years."

Liam's throat tightens so much hardly any air can get through.

"You know our motto?" the girl says. "Are you the kids who saved Egypt?"

Aria and Liam recoil in perfect sync, like they're mirroring each other. How could she know about them?

To Aria's knowledge—and she spent hours digging through old books in the Sommetville library—their time in Egypt was never recorded anywhere. She was disappointed about it. They'd risked their lives to save Ramesses II and his kingdom! They deserved some credit.

A smile spreads across her face. Maybe their story made it through time after all. Not all history leaves a paper trail.

"Yes, it was us," Aria says with forced modesty. "We helped Ramesses II. No big deal."

"*No big deal?*" Liam blurts out, his higher-than-normal voice echoing off the walls.

Aria presses a finger to her lips and hushes him so sharply that a tiny spray of spit lands on Liam's nose.

"I'm so glad you're here," the girl says. "I heard all about your adventure in Egypt from a storyteller, and I just knew you would come to help me save Rome. I wasn't sure you were real, or if any of the story was true, but I had to try to find you. That's why I asked the god Janus, who presides over the beginning and ending of conflict, for help."

Liam's brows furrow like an old man's. Their adventure in Egypt was intense. He didn't like it at first, and if he had the choice, he probably would have quit. But after a while, he got used to it, and the thrill of the adventure began to win him over. Worse still, the more dangerous it became, the more alive he felt. Not that he could ever admit that to Aria. She'd only drag him into more dangerous situations, and he loves his life far too much to gamble it away.

So doing it all over again? That's a different story. They almost died last time!

And now, the moment they arrive somewhere new, someone's already trying to kill them. Why would he risk his life for strangers again?

THREE
THE RULES

Wedged between the haystack and Aria, Liam leans forward to lock eyes with the girl. "Sorry, but who are you?"

"Oh! Where are my manners? I'm Gaia. My father is Tiro Carina. He's a Senator. And this is my dog, Aello." She gestures at the tiny furball curled up on her crossed legs.

Liam grimaces at the dog, and Aria stifles a laugh. There's a certain joy in watching her best friend squirm. She never understood why, but for as long as she's known him, Liam has always been afraid of small animals. He could shake paws with a bear, but a rabbit would send him running.

"Nice to meet you, Gaia. I'm Aria, and the weird one

here is my best friend, Liam. Why did you call us? And why are those men chasing you?"

Gaia's eyebrows pull together. "That's the thing. I don't know why those men were after me." She glances in every direction, then leans closer to Aria and Liam. "Rome isn't what it used to be. It's not safe anymore," she whispers. "I was with my friend Titus at our usual meeting place, not far from where I found you. Titus is..." She looks down at Aello and pats her fur a few times. "Titus doesn't have the same social status as me anymore. That's why we meet in secret. No one from my circle can see us together."

"Wait," Liam cuts in. "You mean just because you're not in the same social class, you can't hang out with him?"

Gaia nods. "My parents would never allow it, especially after what happened to his family."

Liam's eyes bulge as he says to Aria, "What the heck is this place?"

"Calm down," Aria says. "This isn't Sommetville. Things were different back then."

"Yes, but—" Liam cuts himself off when he sees Aria's reproachful glance. He sighs. "Sorry, Gaia. I got carried away. I'm listening now."

Aria smiles with such satisfaction that Liam wishes he could wipe it off her face.

Gaia clears her throat. "Thank you. Titus and I were sitting on our bench, talking like always. It was getting late, so I had to get back home if I didn't want my mother to get suspicious. She knows what time school finishes. Not even five minutes into my walk back, those two guards started chasing Aello and me."

She pets her dog. "And luckily, even with her short legs, she runs like a cheetah."

Liam opens his mouth to comment, but Gaia is faster. "Then I saw you. When I noticed how strangely you were dressed, I knew you must be the duo from the future, coming to help me. You showed up just in time."

"How fabulous for us," Liam mutters, but a shrill horse's neigh drowns out his remark.

"Can you believe it, Liam?" Aria beams like she's just won the lottery—again. "We're so famous now that we get called all across history to save the world!"

"But why us?" Liam asks. "It's not like we're the best at anything."

Gaia scoops Aello into her arms and stands up. "I can't give you an answer, but we should head to my house before the men find us. I'll explain everything about the mission on the way, but first, we need to find clothes for you two. You can't walk around dressed like that. People will get suspicious."

"Listen," Liam says, "I'm sure you're a really nice girl, but I'm getting tired of people wanting us to change our outfits every time we're asked to help them."

"Don't worry, Liam," Aria says, batting her eyelashes at him. "This time you won't need makeup, just a dress." She presses her lips together, trying not to laugh.

"You can keep your clothes if you want," Gaia says. "But if you stand out too much, there's a greater risk you'll get arrested, and I doubt you'd enjoy prison or the arena."

Liam gulps. "Okay, point taken. I'll stay low-key. I've got a soccer game this weekend, and I plan to win. So bring on the dress."

"Perfect." Gaia puts Aello on the ground. She pulls a few silver coins from a pouch attached to her belt and gives her dog instructions. Aello takes the coins in her mouth, biting down with her sharp canines, then trots off toward the merchant street.

"What is she doing?" Liam asks, completely baffled.

"She's buying you some clothes," Gaia says matter-of-factly. "I'd go, but I'm worried those men might still be nearby."

"But how can she manage? She's just a dog," Liam says. He shakes his head in disbelief, a feeling that only grows when the dog returns with one piece of green and one piece of yellow fabric clutched in her teeth.

Gaia hands Aria and Liam a tunic; the longer green one is for Aria and the shorter yellow one for Liam. "Here you go. Not the fanciest, but they'll do until we get to my house."

Liam unfolds his tunic—a pastel-yellow rectangle with a rounded collar. He can tell that when he puts it on, the hem will come to his knees. With no pockets and no embellishments, the outfit is definitely more Spartan than stylish. And where is he supposed to hide his phone? He's not giving that up.

Aria slips her tunic on over her gym clothes. The dark red of her Sommetville Junior High tee still shows faintly through the light shade of green linen, but the loose fit helps her school clothes blend in.

"Smart," Liam says, and puts his tunic on over his gym clothes too.

Liam looks down and sighs with relief. His tunic is so sheer, he's glad he has something on underneath. His gym clothes are saving him from embarrassment.

Gaia smiles at them, but her expression tenses when her gaze drops to their white sneakers. "We'll find you proper footwear on the way. I know the best shoe shop in town. They sell sandals made from the finest papyrus leather. You'll love them."

"I'm sure I will," Liam says through clenched teeth.

Gaia heads out from behind the haystack and adds, "Stay close to me so I can tell you why you are here, and let's keep our voices down. You never know who might be listening."

"Did you hear that, Aria? Try not to *scream* when you talk," Liam says, winking.

"How dare you? You've been shouting like we're deaf ever since we got here."

"I'm sorry for being shocked that we're once again stranded thousands of years in the past," Liam says, his voice rising.

"Shh!" Gaia and Aria say.

Liam zips his mouth shut, twists an imaginary lock, and tosses the key over his shoulder.

After making sure no men in armor are waiting for them around the corner, they turn onto the main avenue. Aello takes the lead, and despite her tiny size, the furry, four-legged creature struts like she owns the city.

The scents of spices and baked bread drift from nearby food stalls, giving Liam a moment of comfort. He takes a deep breath. As the familiar aromas fill his nose, he closes his eyes and for a second, it feels like he's back in Sommetville, standing in front of Baguetteville, the best bakery in town.

The group weaves through the lively city, every step carrying them deeper into another world. Aria's mind spins in a hundred directions. The noise, the smells, the crowds—it's all too much. She tries to focus on Gaia's words, but her attention keeps slipping to her surroundings.

Then she hears one word Gaia is saying. It's six letters long, and it brings her back to the conversation.

Her blood runs cold as the word *murder* echoes through her mind.

FOUR
THE MISSION

Gaia stops in front of a house that appears to double as a shoe shop. Two tables outside the front door are covered with all kinds of sandals—some plain brown, some black, others decorated with tiny gemstones woven into the straps.

She picks up a basic brown pair and holds it next to Aria's foot. "These should fit you."

She does the same for Liam, and they swap their comfy sneakers for open-toed sandals. Liam wiggles his left foot and tugs at the two pieces of papyrus that look like shoelaces attached to the sides of his new sandals. He glances at Aria, who's busy wrapping the laces around her shin and tying them in a bow. He copies her. When he finishes, he stands and looks proudly at his legs.

"More comfortable than I expected," he says, surprised.

A man comes out of the store and says, "Five hundred denarii."

"Here you go," says Gaia, and she hands him the coins.

As they walk away, Aria leans closer to Gaia. "You were saying your friend Titus learned about a plot to murder someone?"

"Yes. He delivers wine barrels to a tavern, and he overheard two men talking about it."

"Do you know who they want to assassinate?" Liam asks.

"Julius Caesar."

Aria covers her mouth to suppress a gasp.

Liam turns to his best friend. "Wait, isn't that a Roman senator we learned about a couple of weeks ago?"

Aria only manages a nod.

"But isn't he a bad guy?" Liam says. "Aren't the senators keeping all the riches for themselves and abusing their powers, so they feel better about themselves?"

Aria looks up at the sky, as if pleading for help. "Liam, it's not our place to decide who should live or die.

From what we know, Caesar was loved by the Romans, and he wasn't the worst person of his time. The citizens of Rome placed a lot of hope in Julius Caesar. According to history books, he defended the rights of common people and wanted to limit the power of aristocrats."

"Really?" Liam asks. "I should probably start paying attention in class," he mumbles, mostly to himself. He feels Aria's glare and adds, "Sorry, keep going."

"What came after his death was terrible for Rome. Maybe things wouldn't have been perfect if he'd lived, but honestly, I can't see how they could've been worse."

Gaia stops walking. "What do you mean?"

Aria's face tightens. Why does she always get stuck delivering the bad news?

She knows she won't receive any help from Liam to answer Gaia's question. They had the lesson on Julius Caesar a month ago, but he slept through it. Aria was so annoyed, she drew cat whiskers on his cheeks with her black pen in revenge. He woke up furious and later had to come up with an excuse to explain his face decorations to his mom.

Aria hesitates, then begins, "As I was saying, most Romans *loved* Caesar. But not everyone felt the same. Some senators supported him, but many hated him because they didn't want to lose their privileges. We don't know who betrayed him, but Julius Caesar was murdered. After that, a wave of terror swept through Rome. The poor lost their rights and were treated like slaves. Rome never really shone again once he was killed."

Gaia turns ashen. "That's awful," she whispers.

"But we can fix it," Aria says. "Do you have any idea who might be behind the murder plot?"

Gaia glances around and replies in a voice barely above a whisper. "Actually, yes. I think it's Septimus. He's the most powerful senator in Rome right now, and one of the worst. He and Caesar don't see eye to eye when it comes to managing the Empire and distributing resources. It wouldn't be the first time he's wanted to eliminate a rival."

"Okay, but is he so upset he'd want to kill someone? It's extreme," Liam says.

"Unfortunately, committing murder to get rid of a rival is not that rare for this time," Aria says.

Her thoughts begin to drift. Ancient Rome has always been one of her favorite eras of history. But she can't forget how brutal the past could sometimes be. She knows it's unfair to judge people in ancient cultures by today's standards, but it's still hard to understand how they could be so cruel to one another.

"He already committed a murder," Gaia says, drawing Aria out of her reverie. "And he got away with it."

FIVE

THE SENATOR

"What do you … mean?" Liam asks, his voice sounding as shaky as his legs feel.

"Septimus murdered Titus's father."

Aria's eyes fly wide as she draws in a startled breath. "How do you know?"

Gaia moves forward again. "It's complicated, and I can't risk someone overhearing us here. I'll tell you once we're at my house. But Titus wasn't always poor, far from it. His family used to be richer and more powerful than mine, in fact. Let's keep walking."

The streets have no sidewalks, so everyone walks down the center, stepping aside when a horse pulling a cart passes through.

Until she can learn more about the plot threatening one of the most famous people in history, Aria finds comfort in the beauty around her. The city looks just as she imagined it.

Her eyes shine when she spots the Capitoline Hill, the religious heart of Rome dedicated to Jupiter, Juno, and Minerva. At its summit stands the majestic Temple of Jupiter Optimus Maximus. Tall white marble columns rise toward the sky, supporting a richly decorated pediment. Figures of the gods—Jupiter at the center, with Juno and Minerva beside him—stand above the entrance as if guarding the city.

"Liam, do you have your phone? Mine was in my backpack. I want to take a picture of the Temple of Jupiter."

"Are you kidding?" Liam replies, exasperated. "Did you *not* hear what Gaia just said? We have a killer on the loose, and you want to play tourist? Besides, I can't charge my phone here, and we might need it later. If we ever want to get home, we need to focus."

"Okay, okay," Aria sighs.

Gaia looks at Aria and Liam in turn. "Does this mean you will help Titus and me save Caesar?"

Liam's shoulders sag in resignation. Risking his life again for people he doesn't even know feels foolish, annoying even. But can he live with himself if he doesn't try? He lets the silence hang for a moment before saying, "We can try."

"We have to do better than try," Aria says. "I don't think we can go home until we save Caesar."

Liam lifts his arms overhead, then lets them fall to his sides. "Aria, can you at least pretend this is our decision and not something being forced on us?"

Aria rolls her eyes. "Oh, come on, Liam. Why do you always have to play the victim? We're lucky to be here!"

"Thank you," Gaia cuts in, as if rushing the words will keep them from changing their minds. "My house isn't far; we will be there in no time."

"Do your parents know Caesar?" Aria asks.

"Yes, my father is close to him. They are both senators, and they share the same political beliefs."

"So why not ask your father for help?" Liam says.

"I tried. I went to my father and told him that I'd overheard a plot to kill Caesar. I couldn't mention Titus, of course. But he didn't believe me. He thinks Caesar is too popular and no one would dare attack him. And despite my father's differences with Septimus, he is friends with him. He refuses to see what he's really like."

"Septimus is the one you think killed Titus's father and who wants to kill Caesar, right?" asks Liam, and Gaia agrees. "But if Titus has proof that Septimus murdered his father and he brings it to your dad, I am sure they will order his arrest and Caesar will be saved in the process."

Gaia steps in front of Aria and Liam, blocking their path. Fear sharpens her features as she raises a trembling finger to hush them. "You can never tell anyone I'm still friends with Titus. If someone found out, I'd be in serious trouble, and I won't be able to help him anymore. He depends on me to eat most days."

"Okay, don't worry. We won't say anything," Liam says. "But I don't get why Titus has to hide just because his father was killed. It's awful, and not his fault. If Septimus is guilty, he should pay. Why isn't anyone doing anything?"

"He didn't kill him directly. The truth is even more sinister," Gaia says.

Aria's eyebrows knit together. "What do you mean?"

"Septimus framed Titus's father for a scam he never committed. He was sent to prison and forced to fight the most powerful gladiator in the world."

"That's how he died?"

Gaia nods, her eyes shimmering with tears.

Aria pats her arm. "We'll do everything we can to stop Septimus from harming Caesar. And if we can, we'll find proof that Titus's father is innocent. Won't we, Liam?" She lifts an eyebrow at him.

Liam hesitates before saying, "We will. If Titus's father is really innocent, of course."

"Thank you, and he is!" Gaia replies.

"If you say so," Liam says. "Where should we start?"

"Titus and I already snuck into Septimus's house and searched his home office, but we didn't find any evidence that could incriminate him for the murder plot or the scam. It's not surprising. He probably doesn't keep important information at his home office, since it isn't as secure as his office at the Senate."

"So you think we should look in his office at the Senate?" Aria asks.

"Yes, but as I said, it's heavily guarded, so we need to be clever about how we do it."

"It'll be fine," Aria says. "Liam and I are experts at breaking the rules and getting into places we're not supposed to be."

Gaia beams. "I knew you were the perfect people for this mission."

Liam tries to keep his voice steady as he asks, "How guarded is the Senate, exactly?"

"At least one guard per senator," Gaia replies. "If my

information is correct, one is stationed in front of Septimus's office at all times."

A knot forms deep in his chest. Once again, Aria might be too optimistic about what they can accomplish.

"Liam, be careful!" Aria grabs his arm and pulls him aside just in time to avoid a passing horse and rider.

"We'd better hurry. I should've been home a long time ago, and my mother will be worried," Gaia says.

SIX

THE CARINAS

As if under a spell, Aria and Liam lose all sense of time as every turn on their journey to Gaia's house reveals more of the city's splendor. Grand temples come into view, then give way to private villas that look like they belong on an ancient postcard.

Liam studies the sprawling homes, impressed by what ancient Romans could build without modern technology. The walls may block curious eyes, but the houses are so massive their red-tiled roofs rise above them. Each place looks at least five times bigger than his own house.

Aello dashes ahead to a pair of arched metal doors flanked by protective walls. Her tail wags faster the closer she gets. She stops in front and waits for Gaia.

The moment she catches up, her mistress scoops her up. "We've arrived," Gaia says to Aria and Liam.

She lowers her voice. "I'll tell my mother you're students from Alexandria here on an educational trip. We'll say we met at school, and I invited you to stay so you could experience real Roman life. She'll love showing off our customs."

"Okay, great," Aria says. "I think I know enough about Alexandria in case she asks something."

A metal doorknocker in the shape of a lion's head is affixed to one of the doors. Gaia seizes the metal ring clamped in the animal's mouth and bangs it loudly. A shrill screech of rusted metal fills the air as both doors creak open. A man appears, so tall and broad that he blocks the whole doorway by himself.

One look at him, and Liam instantly understands why Gaia didn't argue when her father dismissed her concerns about Septimus. You'd have to be *insane* to challenge a guy as big as him. If Liam had a father that intimidating, he'd never talk back either.

"H-hi … Mr. Carina. I'm … Liam. It's nice to meet you," Liam stammers, offering a shaky handshake and silently hoping the man doesn't crush his fingers.

Gaia and Aria burst out laughing as Liam shrinks under the man's intense stare.

Aria leans in and whispers, "He's not Gaia's father; he must be the guard. You really think the master of the house would open the door himself?"

"How am I supposed to know? I'm not a walking history book!" Liam grumbles, flashing the man an awkward smile.

The bodyguard steps aside to let them through. They walk single file into a beautiful garden, full of lush grass and patches of flowers. The garden wraps all around the house and hosts many kinds of trees and flowers. Everything is arranged so neatly it's obvious a professional designed it. There's even a bubbling fountain on one side.

At the end of the stone path stands the Carina family's house, a single-story building so large that Liam thinks the school gymnasium back home might be smaller. The walls are unusually tall for a house with only one floor, and the steep, pointed roof adds even more height. A row of five columns supports the terrace roof and leads the way to the main entrance.

Before they have a chance to reach the entrance to the house, the front doors swing open, revealing a woman with youthful and delicate features wearing a simple white dress that flows down to her ankles.

"I guess she's not Gaia's mother?" Liam asks Aria.

"No," says Aria, laughing, though she wouldn't have minded watching Liam fall into another trap.

They enter the house and greet the servant, who says Gaia's mother is resting in the atrium. Gaia gestures for Aria and Liam to come with her, and they head that way.

They leave the vestibule and step into a room as wide as the house itself, divided by furniture into separate living areas, almost like a loft. By modern standards, it would be a living room, though even Aria isn't sure what the Romans call it. *I can't know everything,* she reminds herself, pushing away the guilt.

Red and black designs are inlaid in the stone flooring, which stretches out beneath their feet like a giant board game. At both ends of the room are arrangements of couches and armchairs, creating two seating areas. Marble tables stand in the center of the seating areas, each holding a bust, three-dimensional portraits of people long gone.

The walls are covered with bright-green tiles decorated with yellow leaf shapes. Inside each leaf is a red rectangle with a white circle in the middle. The ceiling repeats the same patterns. There is so much to take in that Liam feels a headache forming.

They move to the next room. The walls are painted in the same color palette as the previous room. Tall columns rise around a square opening in the roof that lets in sunlight. Beneath it, a shallow pool of water gleams in the center of the floor, ready to catch the rain.

Along one side of the space, a stone bench sits between two columns, and a woman rests there on soft yellow cushions, watching quietly as the water reflects the sky above. A servant stands beside her, moving a large feather fan up and down to cool the air.

The sound of their footsteps on the mosaic floor draws the woman's attention, and she looks straight at them.

"Mother, I want to introduce you to my friends," Gaia says with enthusiasm, though a hint of fear edges her voice. "They're visiting from Alexandria. They're in my reading class and want to learn more about Rome."

Gaia's mother leans on her arm to rise from the divan. With the grace of a dancer, she lowers her feet to the floor and sits up. Her emerald gaze sparkles beneath her sun-kissed golden hair, the same shade as Gaia's. Her features are fine and smooth, and a flowing cream dress cinched with a jeweled belt hangs from her slender frame. A silver diadem rests on her head, and a necklace of rubies and diamonds adds the perfect sparkle to her outfit.

Her beauty is undeniable, heightened by the warm, graceful smile she offers to Aria and Liam.

"I didn't know your school was welcoming friends from Egypt. What a lovely surprise," Gaia's mother says as she stands and opens her arms to greet the visitors. "My name is Marcia. Welcome to Rome. Gaia never brings friends home, so you must be very special."

"Thank you, Mrs. Carina. I'm Aria, and this is Liam. It's a pleasure to meet you. We've come a long way and are excited to experience Roman life."

"You won't be disappointed. There are so many things to do and see in Rome. You must stay with us so we can show you everything the city has to offer. And I'd love to learn more about Alexandria. I've heard wonderful things but haven't had the chance to visit."

Her enthusiasm makes Liam uncomfortable. If he has to talk about a city he knows nothing about, things could get complicated.

"We'll be happy to tell you all about life in Alexandria," Aria says, which only increases Liam's nervousness. What is she doing?

"Excellent. I'll have someone bring extra bedding to Gaia's room for you. I'm sure she's already told you that we're hosting a large party tonight. It will be the perfect chance to meet some locals and have a bit of fun." She claps her hands with a smile that reminds Liam of a kid at Christmas.

"Thank you so much for your hospitality, Mrs. Carina. Liam and I look forward to it," Aria says.

Marcia smiles at Aria, but Liam sees the wrinkles around her mouth tighten when she turns her attention to him. "Are you all right?" she asks.

Liam nods in silence.

"I hope we will get to hear your voice at some point during your stay," she adds with a chuckle that sounds fake. Liam shivers. She seems like someone who's trained herself to hide her real emotions behind a polished facade.

"Sorry. I'm just tired," he mumbles.

He breathes a sigh of relief when Gaia tells her mother they will be going to her room to rest until the party.

If all the guests are anything like her mother, figuring out who to trust won't be easy.

SEVEN

THE SCAM

Gaia leads her guests through the villa, passing through rooms and turning down corridors. It feels like a maze in an amusement park.

"Wow, this place is huge," Liam says as his eyes adjust to the bold red paintings in the hallway, which are a stark contrast to the yellow ones in the last room they walked through. The villa is stunning, but with all the columns, statues, and artwork, it's too much. He once thought his home was too extravagant. He might have to reconsider.

"You think so?" Gaia asks. "My mother wishes it were bigger. But the location is great, so I don't think we'll move anytime soon."

Her bedroom is just as grand as the rest of the house.

In the center stands a dreamy canopy bed. Large windows on two of the walls fill the space with natural light and offer a breathtaking view of the back garden, which bursts with leafy trees and multiple statues flanked by flowerbeds.

"Your mother seems nice," Aria says. "I still can't believe your parents let you learn how to read."

"Why wouldn't they?" Liam asks.

"In ancient Rome, girls didn't go to school," Aria explains. "Only boys learned to read, write, and study. Girls were taught how to manage a household and be good mothers."

"I know. I'm lucky," Gaia admits. "But it wasn't my mother's idea. My father believes I should learn to read and count, just like the boys. My mother thinks I should only take household classes. She keeps telling him I'll never know how to take care of a home or find a husband if I keep going to 'useless' lessons."

"Does Titus go to school with you?" Aria asks.

Gaia picks up one of the many pillows on her bed and brushes the top, even though there's no dirt on it. "Not anymore. He used to, until…" She pauses, closing her eyes for a moment. Then she pats the cushion. "Before his father was framed."

"What happened to him?" Aria says.

A maid enters the bedroom, followed by two men carrying small, makeshift beds. They set the bedframes on the floor and place a thin mattress on each one. The room is so spacious that the new furniture barely takes up any space.

The maid lays out sheets and tucks in the covers, then turns to Gaia.

"There you go, Miss Gaia," she says. "Your mother asked me to tell you your father is home, and the guests will arrive soon. Do you need help getting ready?"

"No thank you, Faustina. I'll wear this dress."

"You know your mother would prefer something a bit more…"

"Luxurious. I know," Gaia says. "But I don't really care. If she's not happy, that's her problem."

"As you wish, Miss Gaia," Faustina replies with a small bow before leaving the room.

Aria and Liam glance at each other, suddenly unsure of their appearance. Neither wants to make a bad impression.

Gaia seems to notice their unease and says, "Don't stress—you both look great." She runs to her wardrobe, which overflows with dresses and accessories. "Just add these belts. They'll give your outfits a little extra flair."

"Thanks," Aria says as she puts on a light-brown

leather belt threaded with shells. "I know it's hard, but can you tell us more about the scam? We can't be sure, but the two events might be linked."

"The scam was blackmail," Gaia explains. "Senators were sent letters demanding money, and if they didn't pay, their secrets would be exposed."

Liam winces. "So the blackmailer knew things that were bad enough to get paid for his silence?"

"Yes," Gaia replies.

"Was your father blackmailed?" Aria asks, and Gaia shakes her head.

"Did they have proof against Titus's father?" Liam questions.

"Yes, Septimus is clever. He planted evidence in Titus's house. Documents with all the senators' secrets and several more blackmail notes ready to be delivered were found."

"And did the blackmailing continue after Titus's father's arrest?" Aria asks.

Despair creeps into Gaia's voice as she says, "No. That only made things worse for him."

"Okay... Do you have any other suspects besides Septimus?" Liam asks.

"No, I don't see who else could be involved. If it's not him, it can only be his son Oliverus. That boy's a menace. I'm stuck with him at school. He bullies everyone in class."

"Oliverus? That name must be reserved for trouble-makers," Liam says with a grin.

"Why?" Gaia asks.

"We have a guy named Oliver in our class, and he's the biggest bully," Aria says.

"Sounds like the one we have here," Gaia says. "Now, let's go before my mother loses her patience. You're probably the stars of the party now."

EIGHT

THE UNEXPECTED GUEST

The living room has been transformed into a ballroom. To Aria, it's exactly how she imagines a royal party would look.

Laughter blends with the sound of flutes and harps. The guests' bright outfits add even more color to a room that already has plenty. To Liam, it feels like standing inside a painting where the artist used every shade on the palette.

Men and women mix in small groups and argue passionately, as if the fate of the world hangs on their words.

Baskets overflowing with fruit sit on every table. Sweet pastries glisten with sugary glaze, and the air is filled with the mouthwatering aroma of roasted meats.

Servants in simple cream tunics weave through the crowd and offer cups filled with wine to the guests.

"Finally, you're here!" Marcia calls out, and she hurries to join them. "We've been waiting just for you. Come, I'll introduce you to my husband, Tiro, and his senator friends. They're dying to hear your stories about Alexandria."

"We are so excited to be here," Liam replies. For a second, he notices Marcia's smile falter. He can't shake the feeling that she isn't his biggest fan.

"Let me do the talking," Aria whispers to him as they follow Marcia and Gaia.

"Don't worry, I will. I'm not suicidal."

Aria stops. Her mouth drops open as she stares in disbelief at what's in front of her. She rubs her eyes, but the scene doesn't change. She's not imagining it.

NINE
OLIVERUS

Aria's body is as stiff as the statue of a woman holding a torch that's right beside her. Liam's brow furrows. "What now?" he asks her.

She points to the group ahead. Liam follows her gaze, then gasps. "No!" he blurts, and bites his lip as several heads turn toward him. He lowers his voice and says to Aria, "How is it even possible?"

"Is something wrong?" Gaia asks from a few paces ahead.

"That boy over there," Aria says. "It's Oliver, our classmate we told you about."

"The one with the gold headband and curly brown hair?" Gaia asks. Aria and Liam nod. "That's Oliverus, Septimus's son. The one I warned you about."

Liam clutches the belt around his waist and loosens it to help him breathe better. "This is impossible. He looks *exactly* like Oliver."

"Maybe he's one of Oliver's ancestors," Aria says.

"What on earth are you talking about?" Liam squeaks, his voice shooting up like an opera singer hitting a high note. "It's scientifically impossible!"

"Yet, here he is."

Marcia pops up beside Gaia, almost as if by magic. "Aria, Liam," she says, "please meet my husband, Tiro, and his dear friends, Caius and Septimus." She pauses for effect, then gestures to the men with both arms, acting like she's introducing famous actors. She points to the object of Aria and Liam's surprise.

"And this is Oliverus, Septimus's son." The boy stays silent, but his sneer speaks volumes.

"Welcome to Rome, my friends," Tiro says, and he raises his glass to them. "We're so glad Gaia brought you. We've been eager to hear more about Alexandria."

"Is that where you're from?" Septimus asks. His voice is so deep it gives Aria a chill. "I love Alexandria. I visited not long ago. Which neighborhood do you live in?"

Liam's face heats as he flushes. His mind races, but the harsh truth hits him: he knows nothing about Alexandria. He couldn't even point it out on a map if his life depended on it. His eyes flick to Aria, who jumps in without missing a beat.

"Near the Serapeum," she says as naturally as she can muster. "Have you been there?"

Liam stares at her in awe. Thank the universe for Aria.

"I'm afraid I haven't. I'll check it out next time I go. Which is soon, actually. I want to see the new bridge they built to connect the island to the mainland. Maybe we could use the same technique for a project in Rome. Have you seen it?" He locks eyes with Liam.

Liam feels the weight of his stare and blurts, "Uh ... yes. Very marvelous."

"Come now, Septimus," Caius says. "Let's not bore our guests with talk about bridges." He looks at Aria and Liam and asks, "So you two are at Gaia's school as part of an exchange program?"

"Yes," Aria answers. "It's called an intercultural exchange. We come here for a week, and after, Gaia will come to Alexandria."

"Wow, let's not put the chariot before the horse," Marcia says. "Gaia has school to attend."

"It's not like she goes to class anyway!" Oliverus says.

It feels like a shock runs through everyone at once. Gaia's cheeks blaze red. Aria and Liam are speechless. This boy is definitely Oliver's ancestor.

Before the silence grows unbearable, Septimus says, "What do you mean, son?"

"She wasn't in school this afternoon. And it wasn't the first time," Oliverus says, his voice dripping with smugness.

Tiro and Marcia stare at Gaia. Flashes of anger flicker behind their calm masks.

"Is that true?" Tiro asks his daughter.

"I can explain," Gaia starts, but Liam jumps in with, "It's all my fault!"

Liam ignores the accusatory glares thrown at him

and says, "I begged Gaia to show me the temple, the temple of…" Liam pauses, racking his brain.

"The Temple of Jupiter!" Aria blurts out, startling everyone.

"It was both of our faults, Mr. and Mrs. Carina," she adds. "We were just so excited to see the city. We're really sorry."

"It's true," Gaia says. "I shouldn't have skipped class, but I wanted to show them one of Rome's most beautiful monuments."

"I've never seen you at school," Oliverus says to Aria and Liam.

Aria nudges Liam to prevent him from saying something reckless. He takes the hint and exhales the breath he was holding.

"We study at a higher level than you. That's why we haven't crossed paths," Aria says with as much confidence as she can, hoping it overshadows the anger and annoyance this doofus is stirring in her.

Aria crosses her fingers that Gaia's school really does have different levels. Oliverus's lack of response is the only answer she needs.

Gaia seems to relax, but then her father says, "I understand your enthusiasm to see the city…" Tiro's expression softens until Marcia scowls at him again.

"But that's still no reason to miss school, Gaia. Your mother and I work hard to give you the opportunity."

"That's right," Marcia says. "You can go to school tomorrow afternoon, but otherwise you're grounded. Your friends will have to find someone else to show them the city or go alone."

"But Mother, please! They're only here for a week, and they can't go by themselves!"

Marcia crosses her arms over her chest. "Our decision is final."

The group stands in awkward silence, as if they'd rather be hiding behind the nearest statue than facing a parental scolding.

Caius clears his throat. "We can't let Aria and Liam, who have traveled so far, leave without seeing Rome's greatest glory. Would you like to visit the Senate tomorrow morning?"

"We'd love to," Aria replies for both her and Liam. Getting inside the Senate is a big opportunity, even though they'll still have to figure out how to get inside Septimus's office.

"Marvelous. Would you care to join us, Septimus?" Caius asks.

"It will be my pleasure," Septimus says.

Jackpot, Aria thinks. Not even a full day in Rome, and their problems are already washing away.

"Would you also join us, Tiro?" Caius asks.

"I can't. I have meetings all morning long."

"We could ask Caesar," Septimus says. "Where is he? I haven't seen him since he asked me about a marble bust of Plato I'm selling. Is he sick?"

"No," Tiro replies. "He said the reform he's preparing for the Senate, the one meant to improve life for the citizens, is taking all his time."

Aria notices Septimus rolling his eyes, though he says nothing.

"I will come to pick you up tomorrow morning at ten," Caius says to Aria and Liam, who thank him.

A woman about Marcia's age walks toward them. "Marcia, I love your new Venus statue. I've never seen her face depicted as being so thin."

Marcia closes her eyes and smiles as if she's just heard the best compliment of her life. "Claudia, it's me, not Venus! Come, let me show you another piece I just received." She loops her arm through her friend's and leads her away.

The senators say their goodbyes to the children, eager to blend into the crowd and forge new alliances.

After all, these parties are more about power than they are about fun.

Oliverus follows his father with a self-righteous smile glued to his face.

These are definitely Oliver's ancestors, Aria thinks. Oliverus is a person they need to watch out for. Because if school has taught her anything, it's that she should never drop her guard when there's a bully in the room.

TEN
THE PLAN

Liam grumbles as they enter Gaia's bedroom after the end of the party. "Those dice weren't even shaped right. Totally biased. Back home, I'd call that cheating."

Aria smiles. "Here, it's called the gods' will. So you lost fair and square."

Gaia laughs, closing the door behind them. "It was a fun game and a fun evening, even if we couldn't gather more information."

"I never thought I'd meet the same Oliver, just thousands of years earlier," Liam says, flopping onto his bed with his arms folded behind his head.

"Thanks again for helping me," Gaia says. "I can't stand him. I don't even want to imagine what he'd do if he ever caught me being friends with Titus."

Ara sits on the bed closest to the windows over-looking the garden. "You need to be careful. People like him can't be trusted."

"I know. And the worst part is, my mother believes everything he says. I just don't get it."

"At least we're going to the Senate tomorrow," Liam says. "If we find proof that Septimus wants to murder Caesar, maybe he and Oliverus will be out of your life for good."

Aria pulls the blanket up over herself. "Right. But we need a solid plan to get into his office without being seen. And we can't both go inside, Liam. One of us has to stay with the senators."

"I'll search the office," says Liam. "Aria can stay with Caius and Septimus; she's better at the social stuff. If Septimus starts asking me questions, I'd probably mess up."

"You can read, right?" Gaia asks him.

"Of course I can!" Liam scoffs.

Aria slaps her forehead. "We're so dumb! You don't know how to read Latin, Liam."

"Crap."

"We didn't think of that," Aria says to Gaia. "Even I can't. I've only taken a few Latin classes, not enough to read much of anything."

Liam sits up and the bed creaks beneath him. "Wait, I have an idea. I can use my phone's translator app. I'm pretty sure it includes Latin."

"I'm impressed. Sometimes you get a great idea," Aria says. "But how do you plan to use your phone without a signal?"

"I don't think I need one," Liam replies, already scrolling through his phone.

Gaia rolls to the edge of her bed to get closer to Liam. She leans over him, squinting at the glowing screen in his hand. Her face shifts from confusion to surprise, as if she's testing out every emotion.

"What is that?" she asks, pointing at the phone.

"A life-saving machine," Liam says with a smile that disappears a few seconds later. His shoulders slump. "The app won't work without a connection."

"I told you," Aria says.

"What does that mean?" Gaia asks.

"It means we need another plan because neither Aria nor I can read Latin," Liam sighs.

"I can send a message to Titus to meet you there in the morning," Gaia says. "He could sneak in through the window and unlock the door for you from the inside. And he can read. That's an even better plan."

"Perfect," Liam says in a cheerful tone that clashes with Aria's next words.

"But Liam, how can we justify your absence to Caius and Septimus? Now that I think about it, I don't know what we could say."

"I could just say I need to go to the bathroom." Liam beams at his own cleverness.

"This isn't the twenty-first century," Aria says. "The Senate doesn't have toilets inside. They're part of the baths in the Forum, but not near the Senate. And even if you asked, they wouldn't let you go alone. They'd worry you'd get lost."

"Aria's right," Gaia says. "The nearest baths are the Thermae Gavii Maximi, and that's still a walk. I guess we have no choice. I'll have to go with Titus."

"But you're grounded," Liam reminds her.

Aria frowns. "Since when do we care? Caesar's life is more important." Liam opens his mouth to argue but shuts it quickly. It might be one of the most reasonable excuses Aria's ever given for breaking a rule.

"It's a great idea, Gaia," Aria continues. "Do you think you'll be able to sneak out of this place without your mother noticing?"

"I'll have to. I can leave Aello here so my mother

doesn't suspect a thing. I'll have to avoid the guard who patrols around the house and climb the wall, which I've done many times before," she says with a spark of pride. "You just need to distract my mother and the guard long enough for me to slip out."

"We can do that, can't we, Liam?" Aria says, not waiting for an answer.

"Great," Gaia says as she jumps out of bed. "Let me write to Titus and tell him our plan." She hurries to her desk and grabs a quill. She scribbles a message, rolls up the parchment, and seals it with wax. She whistles softly, and Aello hops off the bed and comes to her mistress's feet. Gaia ties the note to her collar.

Liam's jaw drops open when Gaia opens the door to the garden, and the dog trots through. How can a creature that looks more like a teddy bear than a real animal carry notes or go buy clothes? *How?*

"But how will she get out of the house?" Aria asks, squinting at the walls surrounding the property. They must be at least twelve feet high.

"She's a professional," Gaia says with the pride only a parent could have. "She dug a hole under the wall, hidden behind a bush. Now she can come and go whenever she wants."

"This is too much for one day," Liam says as he sinks his head into the pillow. All the day's events are still in his mind as he drifts off to sleep like the others.

They don't know it yet, but it will be their last night together.

ELEVEN

THE COVER-UP

The first morning sunbeam falls across Aria's face as she lies in bed, already awake. She stares at the rectangles of light on the ceiling. Her sleep was occupied by a nightmare where Septimus was pushing a dagger into Caesar's heart.

On the bed next to hers, Liam stirs. He yawns and stretches his arms. "Do we have school today?" he mumbles, eyes still half-closed.

"No. We have to save Caesar today, Liam," Aria replies, her tone harsher than she means it to be.

A moment of quietness passes, just long enough for Liam to remember where he is and process Aria's words. "What's wrong with you? Didn't you sleep well?" he asks.

Aria is up and moving. "It's just this weird feeling I have in my stomach. I don't know how to explain it."

"You're not going to start in about your instincts again, are you?" Liam rubs his eyes and tries to wake up more. "Everything will be fine. For once, the mission seems simple enough. We'll be home in no time."

"But—"

"But it'll be fine! Let's get ready. We've got a long day ahead." He jumps out of bed and makes it neatly, just like his mother taught him when he was a little kid.

Gaia steps out of her dressing room wearing a beautiful light-purple dress with birds embroidered along the hem. She puts on a hooded cape, a shade darker than her dress, and fastens it around her neck. "Good morning! Are you two ready?"

"Yes, but are you sure that's the best outfit to climb over a wall in?" Liam asks.

"Getting caught would be bad enough," Gaia replies, "but getting caught badly dressed? Even worse. I'm not sure my mother would have the heart to forgive me. Plus, I need to hide myself once I'm near the Senate, so this cape will do the job perfectly." She readjusts her pearl necklace. "Let's go over the plan."

"I'll talk to your mother to distract her," Aria says. "I'm not sure exactly what I'll say, but I have an idea."

She and Gaia both turn to Liam, who doesn't look

thrilled. Under their combined stares, he finally gives in. "Meanwhile, I'll fake a snake bite in the garden to get the guard's attention."

"Great! I think this is the best plan I've come up with in years." Aria claps her hands with excitement.

She starts to leave the bedroom but stops at the door. She takes a deep breath and rolls her shoulders in circles to warm up. She lifts her chin and opens the door, then walks out as if she is going on stage.

Liam rolls his eyes. "She's really unbelievable."

Aria finds Marcia eating breakfast on her divan in the atrium. Tiro's political duties always pull him away early, which makes Aria's job a bit easier. She has only one person to distract.

After meeting Marcia yesterday and hearing what Gaia said about her mother, Aria has a sense of how to keep the woman occupied for a good amount of time.

She coughs lightly to announce her arrival. Marcia looks up from a plate of grapes on the side table by her divan. Her face lights up when she sees Aria.

"Aria! What a lovely surprise. Come in," she says.

"Did you sleep well? I hope you're not too upset that Gaia isn't joining you today. But you understand why I had to ground her, don't you? Lying and skipping school are unacceptable behaviors."

"I agree," Aria replies. "My mother would've done the same as you. And I didn't come to try to convince you to change your mind," she adds, feigning a shy smile.

"Oh? What is it, then?"

"I was hoping you could teach me how to run a household properly. Your home is beautiful, and from the first time I spoke with you, I realized what a perfect hostess you are."

Seeing the joy sparkle in Marcia's eyes, Aria knows she's picked the right topic. It should give Gaia the time she needs to slip away.

"I'm so glad you asked. You see, in my opinion, homemaking is the most important skill a woman can learn. We've put Gaia in school, but only because her father insisted. I don't see the point in it. I never went and look at me!"

"You're living proof it's not needed," Aria says, matching Marcia's tone. "So, what are the most important things I should know?"

"Excellent question," Marcia says. Her face turns serious. "The first thing is—"

She's cut off by a loud banging noise coming from the sleeping quarters.

Marcia stands and Aria's heart leaps into her throat. She silently prays the woman doesn't go to investigate. If Gaia doesn't escape, there's no way they can move on with their plan.

TWELVE

THE SNAKEBITE

Liam winces until his face is scrunched up into a little ball, and it sounds as if Gaia has stopped breathing. They stare at the bedroom door, which slammed shut a moment ago when Liam opened the door leading to the garden. A draft came through the room and caused the main door to blow closed.

After a few minutes of hearing nothing from the hallway, Liam opens the door to the garden a little more. His nerves get the better of him, and his hands are so damp that he almost loses his grip on the handle.

"Are you going to be okay?" Gaia asks.

Liam shrugs and lets out a big puff of air. "Yeah. I'm ready."

Without looking back, he steps outside. He walks

along the path, whistling to himself, trying to look relaxed. He can feel eyes on him.

He glances to one side and sees the guard he needs to distract. The man is taller than the fountain he stands next to, and his arms look thicker than the trunks of some nearby trees.

Liam does his best to stay calm and focused. How is he supposed to fake a snakebite? Aria has the wildest ideas! Maybe her plan was inspired by their trip to Egypt. In any case, she's going to owe him one after this.

The guard finally looks away, and Liam seizes the opportunity.

Liam steels himself and yells, "Ouch!"

The response is instant.

The guard rushes over. "What's going on?" he asks.

"A snake! A snake bit me!" Liam screams, clutching his knee and letting out a few fake sobs. The sweat dripping down his face helps sell the act.

The guard pulls a long knife from his belt, and Liam steps back in alarm.

"Where is it? I'll cut its head off!" the man shouts.

Liam points behind him. "Uh… It went over there. Into that bush!"

The man charges at the bush and pokes around in it like a madman. Liam suddenly realizes he'll have to explain why there's no real snakebite on his leg. Why does he always end up with the stupid and dangerous part of the plan? All Aria has to do is talk to Marcia. She definitely has the better job.

"I don't see anything," the guard says with his head half-buried in the leaves.

"I'm sure he went in there. He was small and slithered in super-fast. You should keep looking."

A rustling sound echoes in the air. Liam tries to stay composed. He knows it must be Gaia.

The guard hears the sound too. He stands up and runs toward the side of the house. When he reaches the wall, the trees lining the wall stand perfectly still. No more rustling.

Liam stiffens as a cold dread invades him. Out of the corner of his right eye, he catches a glimpse of blonde hair behind a rosebush growing along the wall, about ten feet from the guard. It's Gaia, and she hasn't made it over the wall yet.

They're going to get caught. What if the guard sees her? What will happen to Aria and him? They'll never make it back to Sommetville!

But then, to Liam's shock, the guard turns around and approaches him. Liam watches Gaia vanish over the wall and lets out a sigh of relief.

"Let me see your bite," the guard says.

"No, no, it's fine! Really, I'm okay. I'm just going to grab a Band-Aid from inside. Thanks again, sir."

Liam darts back into the house and slams the bedroom door behind him.

He leans against it, breathless. It feels like a thousand-pound weight has been lifted off his shoulders. For now.

But how is he supposed to survive the rest of the day?

THIRTEEN
THE SENATE

In the atrium, Aria shouts, "I can't wait to know!" at the top of her lungs, trying to pull Marcia's attention back to her. "Sorry! I'm just so excited to learn all your secrets!"

Marcia looks startled by her enthusiasm, but Aria's energy is contagious. She takes Aria's hand and pulls her onto the sofa beside her. "Please, sit down."

Aria leans in close, eyes wide, pretending to soak up every word.

"The most important thing to know for keeping a perfect house is always—"

She's interrupted again, this time by Faustina's arrival. Marcia stiffens and presses her lips into a thin line.

"What is it? I'm in the middle of something important."

"Excuse me, Mrs. Carina, but Mr. Caius has arrived."

The man enters behind Faustina and takes Marcia's hand, bowing low until his lips hover just above her fingers.

"What a pleasure to see you," he says. "I hope I'm not interrupting anything important."

"No… Well, yes… Never mind," Marcia replies.

"Perfect," Caius says, turning to Aria. "Are you ready to discover Rome from the inside?"

"I'm more than ready, sir. It's a dream come true."

"Excellent. Where's your friend?" He looks at Marcia. "I assume you haven't lifted your daughter's punishment?"

"No, Caius. We must give her the best education possible. It's bad enough she barely practices her skills as a housewife. I won't raise a liar too."

"Very well."

"I'll go get Liam," Aria says, heading for Gaia's bedroom.

"Leave that to me. I'll go myself," Marcia says, standing. "I want to speak with Gaia. I want to make sure she understands why she's being punished."

Aria freezes mid-step. She has to stop Marcia. But how?

"Come now, Marcia," Caius says. "I'm sure she understands. Give her some time to cool off. Believe me, as a politician, I've learned it's always better to talk after emotions have settled. Otherwise, you'll only make her angrier."

Marcia sighs, then waves for Aria to go. Without wasting a second, Aria rushes out of the atrium.

That was close.

Her heart pounds as she rounds the corner and runs straight into Liam.

"Ouch!" Liam shouts. "What are you doing here? Aren't you supposed to be with Marcia?"

"I came to get you, idiot! Caius is here. Where's Gaia?"

"Mission accomplished, my dear Aria. It wasn't easy, and I had to use a lot of imagination. Still, I pulled it off like a champ."

Aria giggles. He always turns everything into a tall tale.

"Congratulations. Your ingenuity shows real promise for the future," she says, her voice dripping with sarcasm. "Let's go before someone comes looking for us."

They bid farewell to Marcia and leave with Caius for the Senate. The duo has a sense of ease they never thought possible in the middle of such an important mission.

Caius proves to be the perfect host, keeping them laughing with stories about the silly things he did at their age. It's rare for Aria and Liam to enjoy the company of an adult, but Caius doesn't act like he's above them; he talks to them like they're real people. Most grown-ups are too serious or full of themselves.

The day is off to a good start.

* 79 *

FOURTEEN
THE BREAK-IN

Gaia sprints for the Senate, her sandals slapping against the stones. She draws curious looks as she passes through the crowd. By the time she reaches the Forum, she's breathless and a little wild-looking, but has arrived just in time. Titus is there, waiting along the side of the Senate building, away from the main entrance. She glances at the terrace in front of the entrance and spots Septimus standing guard, right in front of the Senate doors.

She pulls up her hood to hide her golden-blonde hair and block the side of her face closest to the Senate. Titus breaks into a smile when he recognizes her.

"Gaia, you're here," he says, his voice shaky not with fear but with excitement. "Today we're going to prove my father's innocence."

Gaia's lips curl up at the sight of hope shining in his eyes. "Yes, finally."

"The window to Septimus's office is open. I'll go in that way."

"But hurry. I don't know how long Aria and Liam's visit with Septimus will last, and there must be so many documents to search through. I'll go inside the Senate and keep watch. If I see Septimus, or anyone else, aiming for the office, I'll shout."

"But if you shout, you'll attract attention. The guards will see you, and one of your father's friends will recognize you and take you to your parents. You're grounded, remember?"

"That's still better than you getting caught in Septimus's office. And Aria and Liam will be inside the Senate if I need help."

"Are they the ones you told me about, the friends who came to help us?"

Gaia nods.

Titus hesitates before asking, "But can we really trust them?"

"Yes, don't worry. You go find the evidence we need and leave the rest to me."

Titus takes her hands and gives them a gentle squeeze before running to the open ground-floor window.

Gaia watches him climb inside. Now it's time for her to do her part of the plan.

She quickens her pace along the building toward the main entrance, one hand on her hood to keep it in place. Her eyes drift to the garden on her left, where she sees a figure hurrying toward the senators' office windows she just left. Suspicion prickles at her, and she slows. His face is hidden by the hood of a black cape, but the cut of his tunic makes it clear he is a man. He is so gaunt, and his legs are so thin, he looks like a skeleton.

She slows, turning to keep her eyes on him. A gasp rises in her throat as he stops at the exact spot where Titus had stood only moments earlier and scrambles through the window. He vanishes inside.

She freezes. What should she do? Then, in a heartbeat, she breaks into a run toward the window.

She has barely taken a few steps when a hand clamps onto her shoulder and yanks her back.

"I thought you were grounded. What are you doing here?" Oliverus says, his voice full of threat.

FIFTEEN
THE MEETING

Caius bounds up the Senate steps two at a time. He passes between two massive marble columns that hold up the terrace roof, with Aria and Liam right behind him.

"Septimus! What a pleasure to see you," Caius says, shaking the man's hand. "I hope we haven't kept you waiting too long."

"Unfortunately, I won't be able to join you today," Septimus replies. "I received a message from a potential buyer for the bust of Plato in my office. This person is interested in purchasing it and wants a final look." He looks up at the sun. "He'll be there soon. I'd better go."

He turns on his heel and disappears inside the building.

Aria and Liam push down their rising anxiety. Aria

scans the area, hoping to catch a sign of Gaia, but no luck. Hopefully, this means she's already standing guard inside and can alert Titus when Septimus arrives at his office.

Another thought seizes Aria and floods her with fear. Is Caesar the person meeting Septimus? Is Septimus planning to assassinate his target right now?

She tries to remember what she's read about the assassination, but she can't concentrate and the thoughts swirl uselessly, leaving her only with a headache.

"Are you feeling all right?" Caius asks Aria. "You look pale."

"Nothing, just the excitement of seeing the Senate," Aria replies. She tries to sound happy, but her shaky voice betrays her. Caius doesn't look convinced.

Paranoia creeps in. Septimus wouldn't dare commit murder in a place this crowded; it would be madness. Or would it? Who knows what runs through a criminal's mind?

Caius's voice snaps her out of her thoughts. He tells them to follow him inside. She forces herself to focus on the task at hand, clinging to the hope that Titus has escaped and Caesar is safe and far from the Senate.

SIXTEEN
THE INTRUDER

In Septimus's office, Titus brushes the dirt from the windowsill off his tunic, its fabric already yellowed with age and wear. He's worn it for a year and doesn't have the money to buy a new one. Gone are the days when his biggest worries were schoolwork and his parents nagging him with endless expectations. Now, he only wishes he still had parents.

He sniffs, forcing the sadness to stay deep inside. This is not the time to show weakness. This is the time to find proof that Septimus was behind the blackmail scheme. It's the only way to show Rome his father had nothing to do with it and clear his name. If there's time afterward, he'll look for evidence of Septimus's plot to assassinate Caesar. Besides, if Septimus is arrested for the scheme, he won't be able to harm Caesar anyway. A win-win.

When he looks around the office, his jaw drops. Why does anyone need this much space? It's far bigger than his father's office ever was, or any office he's seen in the Senate. He used to come all the time with his father when he was younger. His father believed it would prepare him for his future role as senator.

Busts of the gods Mars and Minerva compete for space next to those of philosophers Plato and Socrates, all perched on columns in the four corners of the room, their stone eyes fixed on him.

In front of the back wall stands a massive wooden desk covered with stacks of parchment, with shelves behind it overflowing with even more papers. The overwhelming amount causes Titus to struggle to hold onto hope. How is he supposed to find anything in all this?

The crunch of footsteps on gravel snaps his attention to the window. He edges closer to get a better look, but steps back when he sees a patch of black fabric looking like a hood just below the windowsill.

A surge of adrenaline courses through him. This person is coming in through the window. Titus needs to hide.

He spots a divan beside the window, not far from the

table. It's his only option. He runs to it, drops to the floor, and rolls under the piece of furniture. From there, he peers out and watches as a man wearing a knee-length cape slips into the room.

The dark figure glides on tiptoe across the room. For an instant, the man turns his head and Titus can now see his face. A scar slashes his cheek, and dark hollows under his eyes tell of a hard life. Titus notices a metal collar around his neck, confirming what he already suspected. The man is a slave.

The figure turns away again and edges toward the office door, pressing flat against the wall beside it. Suddenly, the door swings open, and the man hides behind it.

A second man enters. He has neatly combed dark hair and a crown of ivy resting on his head. His long, white tunic with a deep-red crimson border has so many folds it looks like someone tried to turn a giant bedsheet into an origami bird and gave up halfway through. He glances around with a look of surprise on his face.

Titus recognizes him immediately: It's Julius Caesar. It's been years since he last saw him, yet he looks as if he hasn't aged a bit.

The door slams shut behind Caesar. The intruder

bursts out and launches at the senator with a dagger in his hand. Caesar screams and tumbles to the floor. Titus's head jerks back with fear.

Without thinking, Titus rolls out from under the divan, pushes to his knees, and springs to his feet. He's so quick and silent that the attacker doesn't notice him. Titus yanks the man off Caesar, but the attacker is taller and, despite his thin appearance, stronger. He quickly shoves Titus aside. Raising his dagger, the man lunges at Caesar again, but Titus is faster and slams into him before the blade can strike. With a snarl, the man whirls around and dives out the window.

Titus scrambles to Caesar's side and presses his ear to the unconscious man's chest. Relief washes over him when he hears a heartbeat.

Before Titus can take another breath, the office door opens. Septimus storms in, his face twisting in horror at the sight of Titus leaning over Caesar.

"Titus," Septimus says, his voice full of shock and disbelief. Then he snaps back to his senses and bellows, "Guards! A murderer! Hurry!"

Titus jumps to his feet and bolts for the window.

He runs away from the Senate as fast as he can. A strong breeze hits him in the face, but it does nothing to cool the distress burning inside him as he flees.

SEVENTEEN

THE CHASE

"Leave me alone, Oliverus!" Gaia shouts, jerking her arm free from his grip. Around them, senators pause, their expressions shouting disapproval.

"What are you doing here? I'm going to tell your mother," Oliverus says as he chases her.

"Stay out of my business and leave me alone!"

Gaia stops. The man she saw climb through the window just moments ago now comes back out and takes off running toward the city center.

Oliverus notices her sudden focus and turns to look in the direction of her interest. A boy jumps off a window ledge of the Senate building and sprints across the garden. Three guards climb awkwardly out the office windows and chase after the boy.

Oliverus raises an eyebrow, then smirks.

"He wouldn't happen to be your boyfriend, would he?" Oliverus sneers. "And look, he's being chased by guards too! Whatever he did, I bet the lions will enjoy him for lunch. He looks too small for dinner."

Gaia feels like someone has punched her in the stomach. Her only comfort is that Oliverus didn't recognize Titus. His hair has grown long and is a shade lighter since they were all in school together. Despite all the meals she's brought him, he's lost a lot of weight during the two years he's lived on the street.

What's going on?

She shoves Oliverus again, but he seizes her arm.

This time, her anger gives her the strength she needs to do something. With all her might, she slams her foot into his shin. Oliverus cries out and collapses, clutching his leg.

Gaia takes off after the guards.

"I'll make you pay for this!" Oliverus yells, still bent over with pain.

But Gaia doesn't care. She barely feels her legs moving. It's as if exhaustion doesn't exist. The only thing on her mind is Titus and the guards chasing him.

The farther she runs into the city, the harder it gets to follow the guards. The streets are filled with people, turning the pursuit into a nightmare. Soon, she loses sight of the men. She's surrounded by strangers, and just like that, she's lost in the crowd.

She searches desperately for any sign of Titus or the guards but sees nothing. Her breathing becomes irregular as her worry grows. Tears sting her eyes, and she can't hold them back.

What is she going to do?

She forces herself to inhale and exhale calmly, trying to relax and think. The sun is almost directly overhead. It will be noon soon.

She has to get home before her mother realizes she's gone. If she gets punished again, it'll be even harder to help Titus.

Her heart feels split in two as she hurries back home, away from Titus.

EIGHTEEN
THE ATTACK

Septimus leaps over Caesar's motionless body to get to the office window.

"It's him, it's Titus! Over there!" he shouts to the guards who have come to the rescue. He points to a short figure sprinting across the garden leading to the Forum. "Go after him! Catch him!"

Three guards, armed with short swords and shields, clamber one by one through the window. One nearly twists his ankle when his shield catches on the frame, but they make it out and take off in pursuit of Titus.

Caius bursts into the room with Aria and Liam right behind him. "What's happening, Septimus? We heard screams!"

"Oh!" Aria gasps as her eyes land on the man lying still on the floor. It's Julius Caesar, she is certain of it. He looks just like the marble busts she's seen of him, only with more color, barely.

Is he dead? And where are Titus and Gaia?

Liam kneels beside the senator and checks for a pulse. He feels the faint, steady thump of Caesar's heartbeat beneath his fingertips.

"He's alive," Liam says.

"Caesar!" Caius exclaims. Liam's face twists in disbelief as he glances at Aria, who nods as if to say, *yes, this really is the one and only Caesar.*

"What happened?" Caius asks Septimus.

"Titus attacked Caesar," Septimus says in a shaky voice.

"No!" Aria and Liam cry out together, so loudly that every eye turns in their direction.

"You know Titus?" Septimus asks the duo.

"No, no..." Liam stammers. "We're just ... shocked, that's all."

"It's understandable," Caius says, and turns back to Septimus. "Are you sure it was him?"

"Yes, I saw his face. He escaped through the window, and the guards are already after him. He'll be caught soon."

Aria gulps, trying to hide the torrent of fear, distress, and confusion crossing her face. What happened in here? Did Caesar catch Titus by surprise and force him to attack?

Aria knows how harsh and unfair Roman justice can be, especially for someone accused of assaulting a member of the government or anyone from the elite. If they blame Titus, he won't stand a chance. He'll be thrown in jail, or worse, tossed to the lions in the arena without a second thought.

Caesar groans, as if to politely remind them he's not dead. His eyelids flutter as he tries to open them. He lifts a hand to his forehead and struggles up onto one elbow.

Caius rushes to help, and with Septimus's support, they lift Caesar to his feet. Liam grabs a chair and places it in front of the injured man so he can sit.

Everyone gathers around, waiting anxiously for him to speak.

Seconds go by in heavy silence before Caesar finally opens his mouth.

"Where am I? What happened?"

"We were hoping you could tell us," Caius replies.

"I came in and found Titus on top of you," Septimus adds.

Caesar looks at each of them one by one. "Titus? How—I mean, why?"

"You didn't see him?" Caius asks.

"No. I entered the office at ten-thirty sharp, just as you requested, Septimus. Then I was struck from behind."

"I never requested anything," Septimus snaps defensively. "I didn't ask you to come meet me."

"Yes, you did. And I have your note to prove it." Caesar reaches into his pocket and pulls out a piece of paper.

Septimus takes it from Caesar and reads it. His eyebrows knit together in puzzlement. "I don't understand. It's my handwriting and signature, but I never wrote this, I swear." He digs into his pocket and pulls out a similar slip of parchment, handing it to Caesar. "That's the note I received this morning from someone asking to see my statue of Plato."

Caesar studies it, his expression mirroring Septimus's confusion.

"This is strange," Caesar says.

"Can I see?" Caius asks. Caesar hands him the papers. Caius lifts the one Caesar received. "It looks like your handwriting and signature, Septimus."

Septimus's hand clenches into a fist at his side. "What do you mean?"

"I'm only making an observation."

"Yes, but I didn't write it," Septimus says.

"And when you arrived at the given appointment, Caesar, you were attacked from behind?" Caius continues.

"That's right," Caesar says.

"You didn't see who it was? You didn't see Titus either, only Septimus did?" Caius asks.

Caesar says, "Correct."

"Did the guards recognize Titus, Septimus?" Caius asks.

"I don't know! They're chasing him right now!" Septimus replies, his voice rising higher and higher.

"Caius," Caesar intervenes. "Are you insinuating our friend Septimus is behind my attack?"

"No, no… I'm just laying out the facts," Caius says, his voice too cold to match his denial.

"My attacker must have been a thief, nothing more," Caesar says. "He probably saw the office was empty and was trying to steal something. Then I came in and startled him. That's all. It just shows how badly we need to help the poor. They're so desperate, they'll do anything."

"I'm sure it was Titus," Septimus repeats.

"It can't be Titus," Caesar snaps. "You must be mistaking him for someone else, Septimus. I've known the boy since he was a baby. I stood with his father until his end. Why would he do this to me?"

"Maybe he was looking for something else, and you interrupted him," Septimus suggests. "Maybe he was trying to steal from me."

"Let's see if the guards find him, or if it was someone else entirely," Caesar says, standing up from the chair. "I could use a little rest. I'll go to my office."

"Let me accompany you." Septimus takes Caesar's arm.

"Thank you for your offer, Septimus," Caius says. "But I think it's best to ask some guards to escort Caesar. Nothing personal, but don't you think it's wiser to have him in expert hands, just in case the thief returns?"

"Agreed," Septimus says and goes into the hallway to call for additional guards.

They arrive at lightning speed, as if they'd been waiting for an excuse to be useful. They guide Caesar down the hall to his office as Septimus keeps an eye from a few strides behind.

"I owe you both my deepest apologies," Caius says once he's alone with Aria and Liam. "I invited you to visit the Senate so you could learn about Roman life, and instead, you ended up in the middle of a political mess. At least it shows you how hard this job is."

"Don't be sorry. It's not your fault," Liam says.

"Liam is right," Aria adds, finally finding her voice.

She's still in shock from what they just witnessed and from meeting Caesar.

"I think I'd better take you back to the Carinas," Caius says.

As they leave the Senate, Aria and Liam feel lost. Did Titus intervene to prevent Septimus from harming Caesar? Does Septimus know the true reason why Titus was in his office? And where is Gaia?

NINETEEN
THE PUNISHMENT

Marcia stands in the living room and rearranges a flower bouquet from yesterday's celebration for the tenth time. She hates punishing her daughter and even more, she hates when they are at odds with each other.

Caius was right to suggest giving Gaia time to cool off and think. But it's been hours, and the silence from her daughter's room worries Marcia. Not a single sound. She's probably curled up in bed, imagining her friends enjoying their morning without her.

A wave of guilt washes over Marcia. She tries to shake off the feeling, but no amount of tidying up seems to do the trick. She can't take it anymore.

Determined to regain her daughter's favor, she heads to Gaia's room.

She's pushing the bedroom door open when a mighty crash from the living room stops her in her tracks. She spins around and quickens her pace back the way she came. When she gets there, she lets out an annoyed moan.

Aello is standing by the table right beside the freshly arranged bouquet, now lying scattered on the floor. Her tail wags happily.

"Aello! What have you done now? I didn't see you in here. I thought you were with Gaia," Marcia scolds, scooping the fluffy white dog into her arms. "Well, this is good timing. I was just on my way to see her. Let's go."

She returns to Gaia's room and when she opens the door, she sees Gaia lying in bed, sobbing.

"Oh, sweetheart, don't cry," Marcia says as she heads to her daughter's side and drops Aello on the bed. "I know you're sad about not going with your friends, but you must understand, I had to teach you a lesson. Lying isn't right."

"I'm sorry, Mother," Gaia mumbles through her tears.

Marcia caresses her daughter's wavy hair. "It's okay, darling. You know what? I'll lift your punishment. I think you've learned your lesson."

Gaia sits up and throws her arms around her mother's neck. "Thank you! I promise I won't lie again."

Marcia leaves the room with a lighter heart. She's regained her daughter's trust and her affection.

TWENTY
THE RETURN

Although short, the trip from the Senate to the Carinas' villa feels like an eternity for Aria and Liam. The joy and excitement of the morning have faded, replaced by concern and doubt.

Marcia greets Aria, Liam, and Caius in the vestibule with a bright smile. Her cheerful face is in stark contrast to their anxious expressions.

"Back already?" she says. "Gaia's waiting for you in the garden for lunch, kids."

Aria feels suddenly lighter, and without thinking, she throws her arms around Marcia.

Marcia stumbles backward. "Well! I'm glad to see you too." She chuckles.

"Sorry," Aria mumbles, pulling away. She and Liam rush off and leave Marcia standing there, puzzled.

"Is something wrong?" she asks Caius.

"An unusual event happened at the Senate. I need to speak with Tiro as soon as possible. Is he here?"

"Not yet. He had an appointment this morning, but he should be back soon. Can you tell me more?"

"There was an attempt on Caesar's life."

Marcia muffles a gasp with her hand. She regains her composure and says, "You can wait for Tiro in his office."

TWENTY-ONE

THE PRESUMED MURDERER

Aria and Liam find Gaia lying on a couch at the far end of the garden, shaded by a canopy made of flowing white cotton. Despite the peaceful setting, her eyes are red and puffy, as if she's been crying for days.

She manages a small smile when she sees them.

"Gaia, what happened?" Aria asks.

Gaia motions to the other divan. "Sit down. I'll tell you everything."

They take their seats just as Faustina arrives, balancing a platter of apples and pears in one hand and a tray of bread rolls in the other.

She sets the food down, and the three resume their conversation when she's far enough away not to over-hear them. Aria and Liam lean in to listen.

Gaia tells them everything that happened, including how Oliverus caught her.

"No way!" Aria shouts with bulging eyes.

"Yes. I couldn't get rid of him, and then I saw that man jump back out the window and run off. A moment later, Titus did the same, and the army guards came next. I got rid of Oliverus and tried to follow, but I lost them in the city." Her voice breaks. "I didn't know what else to do, so I came back just in time to see my mother going to my room to check on me. Thankfully, Aello saw what was going on and distracted her until I snuck back into my room." She strokes her dog's fur. "I have no idea what went on inside the office."

Aria and Liam exchange a glance. It's clear Titus must have interrupted the attack and saved Caesar. Could the attempted murderer work for Septimus?

"What? What is it?" Gaia asks, watching their expressions.

After a few seconds of stillness, Aria goes ahead and explains their side of the story. She tells Gaia how Titus has become the primary suspect in Caesar's attempted murder.

"What? I can't..." Tears pour down Gaia's cheeks like waterfalls. "I can't let them accuse him." She stands abruptly. "I have to talk to my father."

Liam grabs her shoulders before she can take a step. He looks her straight in the eyes. "It's not worth it. They won't believe you. And how will you explain being there? Your parents will punish you even more. That won't help Titus."

"I can't let Titus take the blame for Septimus. We all know he's the one who did it!" Gaia shouts, pulling away from Liam.

"We don't actually know for sure," Liam says. "Wouldn't Septimus have stayed with us for our tour if he had known the assassination would take place at this time?"

Aria frowns. "Septimus lured Caesar into his office so his man could kill him. And he excused himself from our tour so he could ensure no one else disturbed the killer and that the job was completed. By waiting for us at the Senate entrance while his man struck, he gave himself the perfect alibi."

"But Septimus looked so surprised..." Liam says.

"Surprised at his luck of finding Titus there," Aria goes on. "His henchman escaped, and now he can blame Titus for everything. With Titus's past, it'll be easy to persuade people that he did it for revenge."

Liam can't deny the evidence against Septimus keeps piling up. Still, something doesn't sit right with him.

When things seem too obvious, he's learned to be careful. "Okay. Let's circle back to the beginning. Why would Septimus want to kill Caesar? What is his motive? Every criminal has one," he says.

"To gain more power!" Aria replies.

"I don't think so," Gaia says. "He's already more powerful than Caesar. Maybe Caesar found out about the scam, or at least grew suspicious, and Septimus needs to silence him."

"If that's the case, why wouldn't Caesar have said something already?" Liam asks. "He didn't seem distrustful of Septimus at all."

"Maybe he's waiting until he has more evidence to make a formal accusation," Aria suggests. "It would be wise."

"Okay, but it still doesn't change the fact that going to your father won't help, Gaia. It'll only make things worse. We'll find another way." Liam feels bad saying it, but it's true.

Gaia sits back down with a look of defeat. Liam offers her some bread, but she shakes her head. "I can't eat anything."

He, on the other hand, can. His stomach aches with hunger. He tears into the soft, fluffy bread, feeling more energized with each bite.

"The only way to know for sure what took place in Septimus's office is to ask Titus," Liam says. He asks Gaia, "Any idea where he might have gone?"

She shakes her head. "What if the guards caught him?"

"Nothing's certain," Aria says, "but if you lost the guards in the crowd, maybe they lost Titus too."

Color returns to Gaia's face. "He's strong and runs fast, so you might be right. If he escaped, he'd go to the abandoned restaurant where he usually sleeps. It's in the rough part of town, where people with good hearts rarely go. And no one will think to look for him there."

"Great!" Liam shouts, his sudden excitement surprising both girls, given the circumstances. "At least we've got a lead."

"Let's go," Gaia says with the same energy.

"Wait, wait." Aria holds up her hand, stopping them both. "Gaia, you have a class this afternoon. If you skip it, your mom might punish you so badly you'll never be allowed out again until you're eighteen."

"I don't care! Titus is more important."

"I didn't know you were such a stickler for rules, Aria," Liam teases.

"There are times when breaking the rules is foolish, my dear Liam." She looks at Gaia. "After your encounter with Oliverus this morning, you can bet he'll do anything to get back at you. You cannot afford to skip class."

Gaia bites her lip. "You're right. But if he doesn't see you two with me, he could also blow your covers."

"I hadn't thought about that," Aria says.

"Aria, you can go with Gaia while I go search for Titus. If one of us is there, he won't look for the other."

"But how will you find Titus? You know nothing about Rome," Aria says.

Aello gets up from her resting spot under a tree and trots over to her mistress. She paws at Gaia's shin, and for the first time in hours, Gaia's face breaks into a wide smile.

"Of course! Why didn't I think of it sooner? Aello will show you the way."

Liam eyes the dog, who barely reaches his calves. She's shown signs of cleverness, but can she really guide him to Titus?

"I guess we can give it a try," Liam says, but he's still doubtful.

Aria gives Liam a friendly slap on the back. "This is a great plan."

"If I don't come back tonight, will you search for me?" he asks his friend.

"Come on, Liam. You know I'd alert the authorities in every kingdom in existence to find you."

"Let's hope it doesn't come to that," Liam says, following Gaia, Aria, and Aello back inside the villa.

They stop to say goodbye to Marcia. They let her know they're off to school and head out to face the rest of their day.

TWENTY-TWO
THE INVESTIGATION

In Tiro's office, Caius sits on a wooden chair with sweeping X-shaped legs and a backrest with floral patterns carved in it. Caius interlocks his fingers and stretches his arms out before him. He's been waiting for nearly an hour.

At last, the door opens. Caius stands up and greets Tiro with a slight bow of the head.

One look at Tiro's tense expression tells Caius that Marcia has already given him a brief account of the reason for his visit.

"Is Julius all right?" Tiro asks, tossing a stack of parchments onto his desk.

"Yes, but it was close. And you know him... He refuses to believe the attack was meant as an attempt on his life. He's convinced the boy was just a thief and that the incident is an additional reason to give more money to the poor. It seems not even a blow to the head can shake him from his mission."

"He didn't recognize Titus?"

"No, he didn't see his attacker, only Septimus did. At least, that's what he claims."

"And you don't believe him?"

Caius fixes his gaze on Tiro. "Caesar wasn't in Septimus's office by chance. He was called there. Maybe Titus was involved, but I doubt he could pull something like that off alone."

"Do you think someone paid him to attack Caesar?"

Caius recounts everything—the ambush, the note, and how he thinks Septimus might have tried to murder Caesar with the boy's help.

"We suspected Septimus of the scam back then," Tiro says. "Maybe he was working with Titus's father, and now he and Titus are working together. Caesar might have discovered something about Septimus, and Septimus wants to silence him before he can act. You know Caesar. He never says anything until he has proof."

"In that case, I'd better go check on Caesar at the Senate. I should stay there too. If Titus is arrested, we'll need to vote on his fate," Caius says.

"I'll go with you. Hopefully, the Roman Vigiles will catch him soon, and he can be punished appropriately for his crime. There's no room for mercy with people like this."

"I forgot some documents at my house," Caius says. "I will go get them and meet you at the Senate."

TWENTY-THREE
MOGURIX

Mogurix leaves his master's home, scowling. His master is mad at him once more, but this time, it isn't his fault.

Not like at the tavern a few days ago, when he talked too loudly with his forger friend about his mission to murder Julius Caesar, and someone overheard. His master was furious—so furious that Mogurix cried the whole night, angry at himself for making such a big mistake.

But this morning's event wasn't his fault, and still, his master blamed him. Mogurix had been sent into a trap. Caesar wasn't alone in Septimus's office, and now Mogurix must silence a witness on top of finishing his original mission. More work. Always more work.

His master was so angry over his failure in the Senate

that morning, Mogurix feared the man would never want to see him again. He wonders if his master might decide to sell him.

Now anxiety spreads through him, slowing him down. His master saved him from misery by buying him as a child, and he loves him so much. He can't live without him.

The memory of his journey from Gabali, his native village in Gaul, to Rome flashes in his mind. He was ten. He remembers the red feathers of Roman helmets poking out from the forest bordering the village, getting closer and closer, until they stood at the gate. Everything after that is a blur. Fire, cries, destruction. That's what Mogurix remembers. It was exactly how he'd imagined the end of the world would be.

The screams of his mother and sisters have mostly faded over the years, but sometimes he still hears them, yelling at him to leave and never come back. Their faces were as harsh as Roman swords. They didn't want to see him again. When he thinks about it, he forces the memory deep down inside himself and it works. The sadness and pain get hidden in the pit of his stomach, where he cannot see them.

His legs wobble, just as they did on that long march to Rome. Then, the Roman guards used their spears to keep the prisoners moving. But above all, he remembers the fear. The fear of not knowing what would happen.

He found out soon enough. In Rome, he was sold at the Forum market for a hundred denarii. That was his worth. He hadn't known then how the Roman coins worked, only that a hundred felt like a small number, almost as small as him.

And after came anger, mixed with insecurity. That's what his first master left him with. But fortune struck when, months later, he was bought again, for even less, by his current master. Instead of fear, he felt love. Love for the man who had rescued him.

Mogurix runs his fingers over the small tag hanging from the metal collar around his neck, no bigger than a coin and engraved with his master's name. A smile spreads across his face as he puffs out his chest in pride.

Yet Mogurix still wishes his master would acknowledge his hard work, just once.

It wasn't his fault he got caught off guard by a kid during the job. How could he have known someone else would be there? He still managed to escape without being caught. But would his master ever give him credit for it? Of course not.

The gaunt, nearly bald man slips quietly through the streets. The morning has already been too long and full of surprises. But he still has a lot of work to do. His master's voice echoes in his mind: "There's been a change of plan, Mogurix. I should have gotten rid of Titus long ago. My mistake. I was too soft."

"Is he the boy who tried to stop me?" Mogurix asked.

"Yes. It's him. You must find him."

"But how? Rome is so big. It could take me weeks."

"I know Gaia brings him food. Follow her. She will lead

you to him. At least there is a positive outcome from the failed attempt of my guards to stop her yesterday. If needed, get rid of her as well. Otherwise, she and Titus might come for me, and we will be separated. They are dangerous."

Dangerous. The word lingers in Mogurix's mind. Nothing is more frightening than dangerous people. He hates this kind of work, but the thought of being taken away from his master and sold again terrifies him. He can never be separated from his master. Ever. He loves him too much.

His face lights up when he sees Gaia with a boy, a girl, and her dog up ahead. Her golden-blonde hair is so rare in Rome that she always stands out. Her parents share the same hair color, though their hair is cut shorter than hers.

Mogurix keeps a good twenty feet between himself and the group. He ducks behind a tree when they stop in front of a door with a sign above it that reads *Schola*. He watches the two girls enter the building while the boy and the dog stay outside.

Who should he follow? His mind races and he feels like he's betting on his life. His master said Gaia takes food to Titus, but how can she do that if she's inside the school?

Maybe the boy is in charge of helping Titus now. Yes, that must be it. He'll go after him.

The dog trots off, sniffing everywhere she goes, with the boy close behind.

They head east and wind through streets that grow more crooked and dark with each turn. Something about the boy's behavior throws Mogurix off. The kid doesn't seem to know where he's going. It looks like he's following the dog.

When they reach the slums of Rome, Mogurix grips the handle of his dagger hanging from his belt, just in case danger presents itself.

Hopefully Mogurix hasn't made another mistake. Hopefully this boy really is going to meet Titus.

The dog changes direction and turns around to come directly at Mogurix.

Heart lurching, he hides behind a rickety vegetable stand. He presses his lips together and holds his breath as the boy's footsteps draw closer.

TWENTY-FOUR
TITUS

Liam has no idea where he is. He's been following Aello for almost an hour and is starting to wonder if the dog actually knows where she's going. They've doubled back a few times, and the unfamiliar streets are anything but comforting.

He probably would enjoy the city's charm if he weren't so lost. Life in Rome doesn't seem much different from Sommetville. Except, of course, for the complete absence of cars, billboards, flashy stores, and the internet. It would be a lot easier to find his way using technology instead of a dog that makes a better stuffed animal than GPS.

Aello barks and catches Liam by surprise. She stops in front of a door and barks again, her tail wagging so fast it stirs the leaves at her feet.

Quick as a flash, she rears up on her hind legs and the nails of her front paws scrape against the weathered surface.

"Is this it?" Liam asks, feeling a little silly—both for talking to a dog and for doubting her skills.

She throws her front paws on his leg.

"Okay, I get it."

Liam's nerves are on edge as he gets closer to the weathered bronze doors that now have a greenish tinge. The purple columns on each side of the doors are crumbling but still standing. What if this is the wrong place and he ends up in front of strangers instead of in an abandoned restaurant?

Liam knocks and steps back to wait. No answer. He gathers his courage and pulls the latch holding the door closed. The door creaks open, reminding him of that moment in a scary movie when the main character is about to be killed. He shakes the thought away and looks in with as much bravery as he can muster.

The room is dim. Old barrels sit in a cluster to his right. A few tables and chairs are scattered around the high-ceilinged room. On his left is a wooden bar, bare on top and backed by nothing but a wall. Above it, cobwebs drape across the beams of a mezzanine.

Liam scowls. This is worse than a haunted house,

and not the fake kind. When he enters, his shoes sink into damp soil. He looks down and sees footprints leading straight to the staircase that climbs to the mezzanine.

Fear slinks into his stomach, fueled by his imagination about all the things this place might hide. After a few moments of eerie stillness, Liam calls out, "Titus? Are you here? It's Liam, I'm a friend of Gaia."

No response. He swallows hard and adds, "She sent me to find you. She's worried about you after what happened this morning in the Senate."

He startles when he hears movement coming from the floor above.

Aello barks again, more urgently now.

Two piercing brown eyes gleam from the mezzanine. "Ahh!" Liam clutches his chest, as if to stop his heart from leaping out.

Is that a tiger? Panic sends Liam's breathing out of control. He remembers the photo in a magazine of a tiger, with its mesmerizing brown and yellow eyes. He even made a comment to Aria about how intense it looked.

But could it really be? *Come on, Liam,* he tells himself. *A tiger would have attacked you by now.*

"Titus, is that you?" He forces his voice not to tremble.

It's hard to tell the boy's age. His delicate features make him look about the same as Gaia—around fifteen —but the faint lines on his face make him seem older. It's as if hardship has stolen his youth. His beige tunic is stained and riddled with holes.

As he descends the stairs, he asks, "How can I trust you?"

"First, I don't think you attacked Caesar. And second, you don't really have a choice, if I may remind you."

Titus chuckles. "Nice to see you don't pity me. But why help someone you barely know?"

Liam frowns. For a moment, he wonders the same. Why should he help someone he barely knows? But another thought pushes in: Why not? "Because I want to. Gaia told us about what happened to your family and the plot against Caesar. My friend Aria and I are here to help."

Titus steps closer. His face is full of distrust, much to Liam's annoyance. He doesn't have time to prove his good intentions. "What happened in Septimus's office?" he asks, steering the conversation in a different direction.

"I went in through the window, and a few minutes

later, another man entered the same way. I hid, and then everything happened so quickly. Caesar came in, and the man attacked him. I crawled out from under the sofa and fought the man off well enough to make him run."

Titus closes his eyes, as if the scene is replaying before him and he doesn't want to watch.

"Did you recognize the man who attacked Caesar?"

"I don't know... No... Maybe. His face looked familiar, especially the scar on his cheek, but I couldn't place where I've seen him before. I can't say if it was in my previous life or in this one. The only thing I know for sure is that he's a slave and he looks like a Gaul."

Liam's brow creases. "Did you just say ... slave?"

Titus meets his eyes, the casualness in his gaze only deepening Liam's horror. "Yes. Many were brought back from the war in Gaul. My nanny was a Gaul. I wonder what happened to her after our downfall... She was most likely sold again." His eyes drift to the ceiling, as though it might hold an answer.

"And you're okay with it? How..." Liam begins, but the rest of the question dies on his lips. Of course he's heard about slavery in history class. Despite what Aria says, he does pay attention *sometimes*. But the idea that one person's life could be worth less than another's is impossible for him to grasp. It always felt like something from a faraway world, almost fictional, not truly real. And yet here he is, listening to people talk about it as if it were nothing. Titus looks at him like he's the strange one, but maybe, in this time, Titus fits better than he ever could.

Liam fights to hold himself together, battling the storm inside just to stay focused. Saving someone from an attempted murder is already an enormous task. But doing it in a time when human life means so little feels impossible.

TWENTY-FIVE
THE NOTE

Standing in the middle of the dusty, abandoned restaurant, Liam breathes in and out slowly until his anger fades. The faster he finishes this mission, the sooner he can return to a time where humans aren't sold like objects.

"If this man has a scar, it might help us recognize him if we see him again," he says to Titus.

"Not really," Titus says. "Scars are common. Parting gifts from the war."

Liam knows history is full of wars, but sometimes it feels like people fought them as if it were some kind of hobby. How Aria can be a fan of history, he'll never understand.

"Gaia and Aria will meet us at your usual spot soon. But before we go, do you know any forgers in Rome?"

"Why? Are you planning to scam someone?" Titus chuckles sarcastically, then suddenly cuts himself off. His face hardens. "You're trying to find who faked the evidence against my father?"

"I wasn't thinking about your father but about the forged notes Septimus and Caesar received. We can ask about your father too."

"What notes?" Titus asks. Liam quickly fills Titus in on what happened after he left the office. He explains he also now doubts Septimus's guilt.

Fury takes over Titus's face as he says, "Septimus is behind everything. No need to lose time searching for someone else. We need to stop him."

"Hey, calm down! I'm trying to help. You all believe he's guilty, but what if he isn't? What if we waste time chasing the wrong person? We can't afford that. We need proof before we accuse anyone. If we go after him and he's innocent, we're screwed. And I don't want to stay stuck here forever!" His voice rises so high it seems to vibrate through the room.

Titus bites his lip. "Fine. I don't know a forger myself, but I know someone who does. We can ask him."

"Thank you." Liam bows his head.

"But how can I leave here? The guards are searching for me everywhere. I'm accused of attempted murder."

Liam studies Titus from head to toe. His curly brown hair, falling just above his shoulders, gives him an innocent look. But his eyes tell a different story—one of resilience and hard-earned strength. His tunic is filthier than anything Liam has ever seen, but the long, cotton brown belt, resembling the ones worn in judo at Titus's waist, gives him an idea.

"Take off your belt. We'll cut it up and make a bandage out of it."

"Are you serious? It's the only one I've got," Titus says, his face screaming, *Don't touch my stuff!*

"Do you want to be arrested?"

Grumbling, Titus obeys. Liam tears a strip from the edge of the tunic, then hands the belt back. He rolls the fabric into a makeshift eye patch. With all the wars raging, Titus will look less like a criminal and more like a wounded warrior.

Liam puts his hands on his hips and gives Titus a final once-over. "I think you're ready to go outside."

"If you say so. Let's go." Titus heads for the door.

Aello greets them at the doorway, where she's standing guard. She seems just as happy to see Titus as he is to see her. After their quick reunion, she leads the way down the street.

They walk in silence, but the quiet makes Liam uneasy. "Where's the rest of your family? I mean, besides your father?" he asks, relieved to hear a voice even if it's his own.

"Dead."

A lump lodges in Liam's throat. Why did he have to open his big mouth?

"My mother and two sisters died of malaria one winter ago," Titus says. He pauses before adding, "And my brother… He volunteered for the army so he could eat. He left for the battlefield and never came back."

Liam has never felt tension this heavy. "That's … bonkers," he says, trying to break the mood but only making things worse. "I'm sorry. I mean … sorry for all of them."

"No need to be sorry. At least now I earn enough at my job to feed myself. And Gaia brings me extra when she can. She never abandoned me. She knows my father was innocent. She has stayed by my side." His eyes glisten, and he sniffs to keep the tears from escaping.

Liam stays quiet. This is more than anything he's ever faced. All he can do is feel grateful for the time he was born into. He can't imagine working a full-time job at Titus's age, or what it must feel like to have so little control over your future. He promises himself to never complain again when his mom asks for help around the house.

TWENTY-SIX
THE LONG GAME

From his hiding spot behind a row of barrels, Mogurix grins from ear to ear. The boy has led him straight to Titus! Even with a fabric eye patch covering part of the boy's face, Mogurix recognizes him the moment he leaves the building.

The two boys don't look dangerous. No weapons, no threat. Getting rid of them will be easy. He just needs to wait for the perfect moment and place. Until then, he'll stalk them.

Mogurix's heart nearly stops when Titus and the boy come toward him and pass just inches away from his hiding spot. He grips his dagger tightly, ready to strike if needed.

Luckily, they don't see him.

He waits until the boys have walked far enough

down the street that it's safe to follow. As the boys rush ahead, Mogurix scrambles to keep up, fuming at how out of shape he is. His breath comes in short, ragged bursts. He loses sight of them more than once, but the gods keep helping him because he always manages to find them again.

TWENTY-SEVEN
THE TAVERN

"It's the tavern over there," Titus says, pointing to the cracked façade across the street.

Liam makes a face that says exactly what he thinks of the building. It doesn't look like a decent place to hang out. The red roof tiles above the second floor look ready to collapse, and the wooden sign, with a carved jar on it, hangs beside the entrance and is just as shaky. Drunken laughter and rough voices spill out to the street.

"I know it looks creepy," Titus says. "But this is the kind of place where secrets pass between patrons faster than drinks. If someone's looking for information, this is where they go. And the owner? He probably knows more about what's happening in Rome than the Senate does. He's in the bar all the time, but his ears seem to reach every corner of the city."

Liam scoops Aello into his arms, and the dog cuddles against him without protest. "I think it's safer if I hold her," he tells Titus, unwilling to admit that the warmth pressed to his chest actually comforts him.

As they enter the tavern, the smell of fermented drinks and spices, mixed with humidity, hits them. Every table is crowded with men tearing into bread and bowls of legumes while drinking their beers. Titus heads for the bar at the far end of the room. The owner sees him and waves him over.

"Titus! What a surprise," the man calls. "Haven't seen you in a while. Thought the city swallowed you up."

"I'm fine. I just have a lot on my plate right now."

"All forgiven, my friend. Better busy than bored in this town. I'm glad you dropped in. I see you brought a friend."

Titus slides onto a barstool and lowers his voice. "It's great to see you, but I won't lie. This isn't a social call."

The owner raises an eyebrow, deepening the wrinkles in his forehead. "You've got me curious. How can I help?"

"We need to find the best forger in Rome."

"Are you planning something you shouldn't, Titus? I

know you want revenge, but are you sure you want to do something so dangerous?"

"It's not for shady business. It's to save someone from a crime. A serious one. The victim received a potentially forged note, so I need to investigate."

"It's risky. You should stay away. You've already been through a lot."

Titus clenches his fists. "I can handle it. So can you help?"

"All right." The tavern owner leans in and gives Titus directions to a house not far away.

Titus thanks him and hurries out with Liam close on his heels. "It's close from here," Titus says.

"Perfect, let's go," Liam replies. Time is short, and he has no desire to spend a minute longer in this place than he has to.

TWENTY-EIGHT

THE SCHOOL

Aria feels ecstatic. This class is nothing like what she's used to in Sommetville. Here, the teacher lets her speak whenever she raises her hand and even seems excited by her energy. It's the total opposite of sitting quietly for hours. In this school, students share ideas, play learning games, and help one another. It's perfect for someone like her, who's always moving, always thinking.

However, Oliverus's cold, smug stares from across the room take away some of her joy.

When class ends, Aria and Gaia are the first to try to slip out. They aren't halfway across the room when Oliverus calls after them.

"I'll see you tomorrow at the Colosseum, I guess?" he asks.

"If you're the one being fed to the lion, I'll definitely come," Gaia snaps back.

"Me? Never. I'm no assassin, contrary to Titus. But what can you expect from the son of a criminal? He'll die the same way his father did. Almost like a tradition."

Gaia's veins bulge at her temples, and she clenches her jaw. She raises her arm to strike her nemesis, but Aria catches her hand before it reaches its target.

"Gaia, don't waste your energy on someone like him," Aria says. "It's too valuable for that."

A weight lifts off Aria's shoulders. She's never felt

this mature before. Maybe this is what being wise feels like…

Oliverus's face turns bright red. His mouth drops open, but he's speechless. Aria links her arm through Gaia's and steers her out of the school.

"Thanks," Gaia says. "If you hadn't stopped me, I think I would've done something dumb."

"It was my pleasure. It felt good to stand up to him. And besides, hitting people doesn't solve anything."

They leave the school and pick up their pace, hoping to see Liam and Titus waiting for them at their meeting spot.

TWENTY-NINE
THE FORGER

In less than ten minutes, Liam, Titus, and Aello arrive at the house of the best forger in Rome.

"Here it is," Titus says.

The building looks ready to fall apart. Cracks run from the foundation to the roof. Not exactly the home of someone working for powerful senators.

"Should we go in?" Titus glances at Liam, whose face is as pale as Aello's fur.

"Uh … yes."

Liam climbs the three steps to the door. On the last one, his shaky legs nearly give out. One step behind, Titus catches Liam's back before he stumbles backward.

"Thanks," Liam mutters as he stabilizes himself. He sets the dog down and knocks.

A man's voice comes from inside, instructing them to enter.

Liam is the first to do so, and it takes him a couple of seconds to adjust to the dim lighting in the room. The inside of the place is just as cold and unwelcoming as the outside. The walls are bare. The floor is littered with hundreds of sheets of paper, each one filled with different handwriting.

A thin, wrinkled man sits at the desk holding a pen, and barely looks up as Liam and Titus take a step closer.

"Thank you for seeing us," Liam says.

"Number of words and a sample," the man replies flatly, not bothering with a greeting.

Liam moves farther into the room. "We didn't come for that."

The man lifts his head and rests his gaze on his visitors. "What do you want from me? I don't know anything. I haven't seen anything."

"I think you can help us stop a murder," says Liam.

"And restore the reputation of the most glorious family in the Empire," Titus adds.

The forger's eyes flick from Titus to Liam. "I don't deal with murder."

"Maybe not, but one of your clients does. And we need his name," Liam replies.

"I don't work for anyone. You should leave."

Liam clenches his jaw. "Look," he says firmly, "I don't have time for games. I think a forged letter was sent to a senator this morning, so he could be accused of murder. I need to know who ordered you to write the note."

"And may I know what this note said?" The forger fixes Liam with a mocking stare that only fuels his annoyance.

"To meet a senator named Septimus in his Senate office at ten-thirty. It was meant for Julius Caesar so he could be murdered."

Seconds pass. The forger's playful look hardens.

A chill creeps through Liam. What if this isn't the right forger? Now the man knows about the assassination plot.

And that knowledge is dangerous.

Why did he think he could trust a man who fakes handwriting for a living?

THIRTY

THE SQUARE

Aria and Gaia walk briskly, nearing the square where they will meet Liam and Titus. Their conversation drifts from topic to topic, but it always circles back to their very different lives.

"Your city sounds like paradise on Earth," Gaia says.

"A little bit, yes."

When they get to the meeting place, Gaia's skin turns a hue even paler than her usual fair coloring.

"They're not here. The bench is empty." She points to the far side of the public space.

The square resembles a wheel with streets coming out like spokes. A row of trees partly hides the crumbling two-story buildings that line the place. Faded laundry hangs from windows, swaying in the breeze. Dust clings to the worn stone street, and the quiet hum of the city feels heavier here. Below a pine tree is an old bench, its wood splintered and faded by time. Gaia and Titus's meeting place.

Aria's blood turns cold. They parted from Liam over two hours ago. Unless Aello got lost, Liam and Titus should already be here.

"Something must have happened to them," Gaia says.

"No!" Aria says, louder than she meant to. "Maybe they just got lost," she adds, as if trying to convince herself too.

"Or Liam couldn't find him! Or, worse, he found Titus, and they both got arrested. They're going to die, and it's all my fault!"

"Gaia—"

"No, Aria. It's all my fault! It was my idea to search Septimus's office. I asked Titus for help. And Liam only went after him as a favor to me." She tries to wipe away her tears, but the emotion keeps pouring out.

"Try to calm down," Aria says, though her own heart is pounding. "Panicking won't help. I know Liam; he tends to take his time. You'll see, they'll be here soon."

Gaia buries her face in her hands, and her words break through sobs as she says, "All this ... for Caesar. I've sacrificed my best friend, and yours, for a senator."

"You did it for the Romans and their future. We made the right choice. We knew the risks."

But Aria's words don't seem to calm Gaia's growing despair.

THIRTY-ONE
THE PLOT

Hidden behind a fountain across from the forger's office, Mogurix no longer knows what to do. He has been waiting for the right moment to go after the two boys, and now they've gone to visit the very man he relies on for all his forgeries.

Over the years, Mogurix and the forger grew close. His master needed countless jobs done, especially during all the blackmail schemes, so Mogurix saw the forger often. So often that he even started to think of him as a friend. There was less work for a while, until recently, when the plans to eliminate Caesar began.

Mogurix taps the pouch at his belt. A few denarii still jingle inside. He could strike now, get rid of the two boys in his friend's office, and then use the coins to buy the forger's silence. After all, it's only fair to pay for the cleanup when you spill blood in someone else's home.

He steps out of the shadows and strides toward the door. Suddenly, a figure in a black cape moves in from his left, walking faster than him. With the hood pulled low, Mogurix can't tell if it's a man or a woman. The stranger stops at the forger's door and knocks.

The forger's booming voice echoes out: "Wait!"

Mogurix slips back into the shadows. Now is no longer the time.

Liam feels the weight of the forger's stare on him as he orders the next client to wait outside.

"I don't know anything," the forger repeats to Liam and Titus.

"I think you do. And you'd better talk, unless you want to end up in prison," Liam tells him.

The forger laughs. "Is that the best you've got? You don't get sent there based on empty threats."

Frustration boils in Liam's chest. He's had enough of this game. He points a finger at the piles of forged notes. "You seem very busy. I doubt you'll have time to clear all this before the Roman police show up. Shame, it looks like a profitable business."

He flashes his best revenge smile. For once, it comes easily.

The forger squeezes the arms of his chair so hard his fingertips turn white. A few seconds pass. Liam knows he's hit a nerve.

"Fine," the man mutters. "I'll help you. But you never met me, and I never said anything."

He stands and walks to a chest by the wall beside his desk. He rummages through stacks of old documents, pulling out scroll after scroll until he finds what he's looking for.

"Here," he says, holding out a parchment. "It's one of the early drafts for one of several notes in the order. I only met the client's slave. The client paid extra to stay anonymous. But this might help you nonetheless."

"Does the slave have a scar on his cheek?" Titus asks, and the forger nods.

Liam reaches for the parchment, but the man pulls it back.

"And remember, you don't know me."

"Of course," Liam says, and the forger finally gives him the paper.

The moment Liam reads the words, his heart skips a beat.

It's a confession.

"Can I see?" Titus asks, holding out his hand.

Liam gives him the paper, the hard look on his face serving as his only comment.

Titus scans the paper and frowns. "Why would Septimus admit to killing Caesar?" He hands the note back to Liam.

"Maybe the better question," Liam says as the pieces start coming together in his mind, "is why someone would want to frame Septimus for Caesar's murder." Liam looks at the forger, who lifts his chin with a grin, as if their confusion is the most entertaining thing he's seen in a long time. "We should go," Liam adds.

Titus does the opposite by inching closer to the forger. The man leans away slightly. "Are you the one who framed my father?" Titus asks.

The forger tilts his head from side to side, letting the silence hang heavy between them. "And who is your father?"

"Publius Cornelius Severianus."

The forger chuckles, biting his lower lip to hold back a smile. "Never heard of him."

"You liar!" Titus lunges forward, but Liam grabs his

shoulder and pulls him back. They are in enough trouble already, and the last thing they need is to anger a criminal.

"You'd better go before I call the Roman guards," the forger says. "I think they would be happier to see you than me." His gaze fixes on Liam.

"Come on, Titus, let's go," Liam mutters, steering his friend toward the door.

He cannot tell if the forger is behind Titus's father's downfall. But one thing is certain now: Someone is plotting to kill Caesar and framing Septimus, setting him up to take the blame and face the wrath of Rome.

THIRTY-TWO
THE REVENGE

As soon as they step out of the forger's house, Mogurix stalks the two boys and their dog from a careful distance.

He's dying to know what they spoke to the forger about. Were they wanting to fake some letters? Or were they digging for information? He hopes it's the former.

His muscles tense as anger rises. He should have tried to listen in. He should have gone inside, done more while he had the chance. What if they're closing in on the truth, just as his master fears?

He has to eliminate them before it's too late.

The boys reach a busy avenue, and Mogurix shoves past people to keep his targets in sight. A group of Roman Vigiles marches by, but none seem to recognize Titus.

That's when a bold idea strikes Mogurix.

Why handle the two boys by himself when the city's guards are already hunting them?

Let the guards catch them. Let them face punishment in front of a cheering crowd in the Colosseum. Watching the two boys fight for their lives in the arena will be far more satisfying than ending things in a dark alley.

He's enjoying the thought so much that he doesn't notice he's standing at an intersection and the boys have vanished. Panic takes hold of him. He can't lose them now.

He starts down the alley on his right, then hears a bark behind him. He turns. There they are, walking in the opposite direction.

And a few feet away, he catches the gleam of Roman helmets.

THIRTY-THREE
THE TRUTH

Once they're away from the crowded avenue, Liam and Titus quicken their pace, forcing Aello to run to keep up.

"We can't disregard Septimus as a suspect just because of what that forger told us," Titus says. "I know he's guilty."

Liam throws an arm out to halt Titus's advance. "Are you serious? After everything that happened to your family because of a wrongful accusation, you're ready to do the same just because it fits your belief?" He lowers his arm but fixes Titus with a stare that says more than words ever could.

Titus looks down. "It's just… If it isn't Septimus, then who did it? He's the only one who hated us enough to do something like this."

"You know what people say—keep your friends close and your enemies closer."

Titus's brow furrows. That motto must have been invented after this era, Liam realizes. "What I mean is, someone could be posing as a friend while working against us. That's the cleverest trick of all, because no one suspects their friends."

Titus buries his face in his hands. "I've spent the last two years hating Septimus. Planning my revenge was the only hope that kept me alive."

Liam gives him a friendly tap on the back. "I get it. And we'll help you find out who really did it."

"I am sure the forger is the one who made the notes that condemn my father. Did you see his face when I said my father's name?"

"I saw and I agree, but we can't accuse the wrong person. We don't know who he's working for, and we need to be strategic in how we handle things. Dozens of guards are after us, and if we're arrested, we won't be able to find the real culprit."

"You are right, sorry. It's just... My patience is running low."

"I get it," Liam says as he starts walking. "Come on, let's meet Aria and Gaia before they collapse with worry.

Going to the forger took longer than I thought, and they're probably waiting."

Titus nods and follows him with Aello at his side.

Liam hears thudding footsteps behind them, heavy enough to make the cobblestones tremble. They grow louder each second.

He looks over his shoulder just as a threatening voice growls, "Don't move, or I'll kill you."

THIRTY-FOUR
THE GUARD

The sound of Aria's sandals slapping against the ground echoes through the quiet square. Unlike Gaia, who sits on the edge of the fountain that doubles as a bath for the neighborhood residents, Aria can't stay still. She paces in tight circles.

A scream splits the air. Crows flap into the sky from one of the side streets and scatter near the girls.

Aria races toward the sound and freezes at the top of the street. Four guards are attacking Liam and Titus.

Liam and Titus try to resist, but they're rapidly overwhelmed. Blades flash at their backs as the guards force them to the ground.

Aello lunges at one of the men, barking and biting at his legs, but a swift kick knocks her aside. She skids across the ground, yelping. She stays to one side and keeps barking from a safer distance.

"What is it?" Gaia asks, coming up behind her.

Aria says nothing. Tears blur her vision until she can no longer see Liam being tied down.

"Stop!" Aria yells. She steps forward but stops when Liam's eyes meet hers. He shakes his head slowly. *Don't intervene.*

Gaia shrieks when the guards drag the boys away with an iron grip on their captives.

Aello runs to Aria and Gaia. She begins jumping at Gaia's feet, but her mistress doesn't move, as if all life has drained from her.

Aria grabs Gaia's arm. "We have to follow them."

She pulls her forward, but Gaia's legs won't cooperate—they wobble like Jell-O.

"Come on, Gaia, you can do it. Think about Titus."

At the sound of his name, a flash of courage lights up Gaia's eyes, and the three heroines chase the Roman guards.

THIRTY-FIVE
THE ARREST

"Ouch," Liam mutters as a guard pushes him forward with the tip of his spear.

Liam can't believe their bad luck. Titus and he were only a few feet from the square when the guards arrested them. How did this happen? They passed dozens of guards on the way, and not one had given them a second glance.

"If you think this hurts, you're in for a rough ride," the guard sneers. "Good thing Rome's full of loyal citizens who know how to find criminals and turn them in to us."

"We didn't do anything wrong," Liam says.

"You tried to kill one of our most beloved senators!"

"That wasn't us," Liam says in defense.

"Oh, you think I'm stupid?" the guard snaps, getting

right in Liam's face. He walks in front of Titus and pulls off the piece of fabric covering his left eye.

"Did you really believe a little disguise would trick us? We're Roman Vigiles. We can spot criminals from a mile away."

Liam raises an eyebrow. Now isn't the time to point out that they'd been walking for over an hour in plain sight, and not one guard had noticed them.

"We want to speak to your superior so we can explain," Liam says.

The guard laughs. "Who do you think you are? The only thing you'll see is the arena, and soon. Don't forget Quinquatria starts tomorrow. And guess what? We're low on fighters. Lucky you."

"What is this quinqui-something?" Liam asks.

The man tugs at the rope, pulling Liam's wrists down and forcing him to lean back to keep his balance. The rough fibers bite into his skin until they draw blood. Liam bites his lower lip so he won't scream. No way he's giving this guy the satisfaction.

"You're a thug, and you don't know the gods? No wonder you're a mess. Move faster!" The guard presses the tip of his dagger into Liam's back again.

The sun sinks lower, but Liam feels like every inch of

his body is burning. Beside him, Titus has not said a word, and Liam worries he might faint from fear.

A crowd has formed on both sides of the street. They're shouting at Liam and Titus, but their voices can't drown out the pounding in Liam's head. How did he go from shooting hoops yesterday to this mess today?

"Where are you taking us?" Liam asks the guard.

"You don't need to know. Your fate will be decided soon enough. With charges like the ones against you, I'd say you'll be the lions' lunch tomorrow."

The four guards burst out laughing, but not with joy. It's cruel, vengeful laughter and it sends chills down Liam's spine.

Liam feels like he can't breathe anymore. Jail? Lions? Until now, he thought talk of being thrown to the lions was just an idle threat to scare people off.

He misses home.

The image of his mother makes the fear hit harder. If he doesn't make it back to her, how will she react? He doesn't need to be psychic to know. She'd tear the world apart trying to find him.

His only hope is Aria. If anyone can think her way out of a trap, it's her. She saw him being arrested. She must already be coming up with a plan.

"We've arrived," the guard says.

Liam looks straight ahead, and this time he feels like he's the one who might faint. The building isn't tall by modern standards, but it stretches impossibly wide. Three stories of perfect arches encircle the structure like a giant stone ring, and on the two upper levels, statues fill the niches between them.

Then it hits him. He knows this place. He's seen drawings, watched shows about it, but never imagined he would see it in real life.

The Colosseum.

Images of gladiators fighting in the arena come back to haunt him. He always thought those TV shows were exaggerated and full of dramatic nonsense added for entertainment purposes. Now he's not so sure.

The guards push them toward a smaller building adjoining the Colosseum, a plain, grim structure with long beige walls, a matching tiled roof, and a tall iron gate that gives the place a nightmare-like appearance.

A deep clank shatters the air and the gate groans open.

Liam digs his nails into his palms. No luck, he's not dreaming. He's really here.

THIRTY-SIX

THE COLOSSEUM

On one of Rome's main avenues, a few feet behind Liam, Titus, and the guards, Aria pushes through people as fast as she can. She can't lose sight of them. The crowd's boos rattle her. They sound more excited and joyful than angry about what's happening to Liam and Titus.

How can people be so hateful without a shred of proof of someone's guilt? And how did they gather so quickly? It's like they were just waiting for the Roman Vigiles to arrest someone, anyone.

"Wait for me!" Gaia shouts. She holds Aello in her arms and pants as she struggles to catch up with Aria.

Aria slows just enough for Gaia to close the gap.

"The prisoners and gladiators are kept in the prison right next to the Colosseum," Gaia says. "It must be where they are taking them."

Aria feels her heart leap into her throat. She loves history, but reading about it and experiencing it are two different things. In books, gladiators were distant ideas: men forced to fight wild animals and each other to entertain cheering crowds. She never felt like they were real. Now her best friend is part of this twisted game.

She hopes Liam slept through their history lesson on the Roman Empire. No point in him being more scared than he probably already is. She vows to find a way to rescue him and Titus before they ever have to set foot in the arena.

"We'll find a way to break in and free them."

Gaia steps in front of her. "Aria, I trust you, I do. But I don't think you get how serious this is. That place is like a fortress. We'll never get inside."

Aria's stomach twists as she looks ahead at the Colosseum, looming at the end of the avenue like the centerpiece of Rome. It's as magnificent as the artist's renderings she has seen in books. In any other moment, she'd be amazed to see inside it. But now, all she feels is dread.

The only thing giving her hope is how strong Liam has always been. He won't give up.

And neither will she.

"I realize how difficult breaking in is," she says in a steady voice. "But we will find a way to get them out. We *have* to."

THIRTY-SEVEN
THE MASTER

Mogurix can't wipe the smile off his face. He's done it. His master will be so proud. He's so pleased with himself that he starts humming a happy tune as he heads to his master's house.

Those two sneaky boys are in jail now, and by this time tomorrow, they'll be lion food after a bloody fight in the Colosseum. That's all that matters. No one will take his master away from him.

He daydreams about how his master will thank him. Maybe he'll buy him a new mattress or give him his own room, so he doesn't have to sleep with the other slaves.

When he arrives at the villa, Mogurix slips into a narrow alley at the back of the house. It's used only by servants and merchants, hidden from the wealthy upper class. He knows how important it is to follow the rules. Belonging to one of the best families in town means carrying a lot of responsibility.

As usual, the maid opens the back door, and Mogurix heads straight for his master's study. He feels satisfied, though the work has left him weary. His eyes drift to the divan.

With no sign of his master, he dares to do what he's never had the courage to do before—sit on the couch. He tells himself he's earned it, certain his master will agree.

The stress and excitement of the day press down on him, and his eyelids grow heavy. His body sinks into the velvet cushions, and before he knows it, he's fast asleep. A sweet dream takes over: his master throwing a birthday party for him, his own room, a trip to the sea…

"Mogurix!"

The shout doesn't wake him.

"Mogurix!" the voice snaps again, and this time it's followed by a smack on the head with a roll of parchment.

Mogurix bolts upright. It takes him a few seconds to remember where he is. When he finally comes to, his master's furious face is glaring down at him, eyes flashing like lightning.

Mogurix jumps off the couch, wide awake now.

"Who do you think you are? How dare you sit on my couch without permission!" his master bellows so loudly that Mogurix refrains from covering his ears.

"I'm sorry, Master. After such an exhausting day, I fell asleep."

"You'd better not let me catch you doing it again. Now, did you get rid of Titus?"

"I did better, Master."

"What do you mean?"

"As you advised, I went after the three kids. The girls went to school, but the boy didn't go in, so I followed him. It wasn't easy. He kept changing direction and—"

"Spare me the useless details."

"Sorry. He went to an abandoned house, and bingo! Titus was inside."

"You got rid of both of them? Good."

"Yes, Master, but not by my own hands."

"How could you kill them without using your hands?"

"They surprised me by leaving their hideout. So I had to come up with a new idea," Mogurix says, though his master's thunderous stare makes him wonder if his plan is as good as he thought it was.

"What have you done?"

"I reported them to the Roman Vigiles! They were locked up in jail in no time." Mogurix puffs out his chest, but his smile fades at the sound of his master's teeth grinding.

His master slams his fist on the desk next to him. "You did what?"

"I … I just … had them arrested."

"I told you to get rid of them without a trace, not hand them over to those vultures in the Senate! What if the senators vote for an investigation and someone questions the two boys? Do you realize what they will say? With your Gallic features and ugly scar on your cheek, you'll be easy to find. And after they're done with you, they will be able to track me down."

Mogurix feels like he's just been stabbed. Sadness rises in him, spreading until it fills every cell in his body. He runs a finger over the scar on his face, a painful reminder of the first time he met a Roman.

"I… It didn't occur to me they might get interrogated, Master," he mutters. "I thought it was a done deal and that they'll be thrown in the Colosseum tomorrow."

"Of course you didn't think! With your goldfish brain, I'm not surprised. That's why I give the orders."

Mogurix struggles for breath, each one harder to

draw than the last. How could he have been so stupid? Because of his own actions, he could lose his master.

"We're headed for disaster thanks to your stupidity," his master says. He moves to the armchair facing the desk and sits.

Mogurix feels his legs about to give out. Maybe he should suggest a solution to win back his master's favor? No. He's too dumb. Better to accept his punishment and let his master decide what is best.

"Did you kill the forger?"

Mogurix swallows his fear. "No, you didn't ask me to."

"Well, take care of him. He knows too much."

His master's order steals his breath for a moment. "We could pay him more to not talk," he argues. "What will we do if we need more forged letters? He's the best in the Empire."

"We'll train someone else. That way, we'll have someone in this house who can do the work." His master smiles. "Now I just have to make sure those kids aren't questioned."

"We could plant evidence against them?"

"With your skills? I doubt it. And we need to take care of Gaia and this unsufferable girl Aria. Gaia has already jeopardized our mission, and once the two of them find out about the arrest, they'll do everything they can to free their friends. They are dangerous. So kill them with your own hands. I don't want to see you again until you succeed." He waves his hand to dismiss Mogurix.

Mogurix bolts for the door, emotions crashing so hard inside him that his head and heart feel ready to burst. He's tired of all the getting rid of people. He doesn't want to do it.

But does he have a choice? He needs his master. He is like a father to him.

THIRTY-EIGHT
THE CRAZY IDEA

Aria can't take her eyes off the entrance to the prison, where Liam and Titus were locked up just minutes ago. There has to be a way into that fortress.

"There are guards everywhere, Aria," Gaia says. "We'll never be able to get in." She hugs Aello closer to her chest.

"Wait, I know!" Aria spins to face Gaia. "I can't believe I didn't think of this before. You see the guards?"

"Yes."

"Well, they take breaks sometimes."

"Yes…"

"We wait for two of them to leave, follow them, and bam, we knock them out!"

Gaia, whose face was showing signs of hope, scowls. But Aria doesn't let it stop her.

"Then we put on their uniforms, sneak into the prison, find Liam and Titus's cell, and free them."

Seeing Gaia's face grow more worried, she adds, "I know what you're thinking—how do we get them out without getting caught? Easy! We write a note that says your father wants to question them. Nobody's going to argue with a senator. No one will be the wiser."

"So you want us to attack two Roman guards, steal their clothes, forge a note, and lie to the authorities?"

"Yes!"

"You're crazy! We'll end up in prison like Titus and Liam."

"How are we supposed to save them without breaking a few rules? Do you have a better idea? We could ask your father, but you keep saying no."

"I don't think we have a choice anymore," Gaia says. "We have to convince my father."

"Are you sure?"

"Yes, and even if it's risky, I still think it's safer than your plan."

"I know mine sounds crazy, but I'm sure we can pull it off."

"Let's go. My father should be home by now."

When they reach the villa, they head straight for Tiro's office.

Gaia knocks, and her father's voice says, "Come in." Gaia pushes the door open, then draws back in surprise before taking a single step inside.

Her father sits behind his desk but isn't alone. Septimus and Oliverus are standing in front of him.

Tiro rises from his chair and fixes the girls with a glare that sends a chill down Aria's spine that spreads to every inch of her body.

They are screwed.

THIRTY-NINE
SPARTACUS

The prison is just as dark and frightening as Liam imagined. The corridors are soggy and sinister. The low, arched ceiling is made of stone, just like the floor. Mud squelches underfoot as the boys are led down a corridor lined on one side by empty cells and on the other by a stone wall. If it weren't for the glimmer from a few torches, Liam wouldn't be able to see a thing. No light. No life.

The guards open a locked door to a new section of the underground jail. As it swings open, a roar of clashing voices floods the space. For a second, Liam feels like he's stepped into the school cafeteria at lunchtime, only this one is full of angry giants instead of hungry kids.

There are cells on each side, all of them packed with prisoners. They stand behind the bars, each one more muscular than the next, like they're competing in a contest no regular person could win. Their faces are scratched and scarred, a reminder of the fierce battles they've survived.

Liam shivers.

"Look at the fresh meat," one of the prisoners says. "Judging by their size, those two won't last more than one show."

The others laugh loudly, and no guards stop them.

"So, who'd you cross to end up in here?" another prisoner asks. His face is crusted with dried blood.

The terror gripping Liam is so strong, he can't speak. How are they supposed to survive this place? Titus and he are tiny compared to everyone else.

A guard shoves them forward, barking at them to move faster.

After the guards let them through another locked door, the noise dies away. They enter a quiet section of the jail, where the hallway ends at a single cell on the left. The bars do nothing to hide the gigantic man seated on the bench inside.

The prisoner's arms are bigger than Liam's head. His legs are so muscular that Liam sees muscles he didn't know humans had. Every line and shape bulges, as if trying to break through the man's skin. He stares at them with piercing black eyes.

A guard searches through a set of keys and when he finds the one he's hunting for, he unlocks the cell door.

"Inside. Now," the guard says.

The two boys scramble to one side of the cell, keeping as much distance from the prisoner as they can.

A loud clang echoes through the hallway as the iron bars slam shut behind them. The squeak of the key turning in the lock sounds like the permanent end of their freedom.

Liam and Titus sit on the bench, silent. Their feet dangle above the floor, shaking. Their faces are covered in sweat. Whether it's from the cold or the terror, they don't know.

Liam glances around his new home. Three thin straw mattresses lie on the dirt floor. The tiny window above lets in just enough light to see and a faint breeze of fresh air.

The gladiator stands up.

Liam presses his back against the wall, wishing he could melt right into it.

"My name is Spartacus," the man says, holding out a massive hand to Liam.

Liam's eyes go wide. One of his favorite fictional TV show characters! Apparently, he's not so fictional. "No way! The most powerful gladiator in the world?" he blurts, forgetting to shake the man's hand.

"Spartacus," Titus repeats beside him, his voice a menacing growl. When he looks over, Titus's nostrils flare as if he's ready to attack.

"What's wrong?" Liam asks. And then it clicks. The way he just described Spartacus is the same way Gaia had spoken of the gladiator who killed Titus's father. Spartacus was that man. "Oopsie."

Titus leaps to his feet, startling Spartacus, who takes a step back. "You killed my father, Publius!" Titus shouts while edging closer, but the difference in their size makes the scene almost comical.

Liam grips Titus's arm. "Stop, Titus. You look like an ant next to him! He'll crush you before you can even say sorry."

"I could, but I won't crush you. I am sorry for your father," Spartacus says with a voice so soft it makes him seem more human and less monster. He goes back to sit on his bench and adds, "He was a truly good man and didn't deserve his fate."

"How can you say that when you're the one who killed him?" Titus yells.

Spartacus bursts out laughing, but it's not the kind of laugh you give when something's funny. It's a laugh of disbelief. "You think we get to choose? The games are planned in advance. Your father knew he was going to die before he stepped into the arena."

"Planned by who?" Liam asks.

Spartacus jabs a finger at the sky. "By powerful men who think they're gods."

Silence falls over the cell. Titus drops onto the bench and slumps against the wall, his body sagging under the weight of it all. Liam sits beside him.

"Which powerful man did you meet to end up here?" Spartacus asks.

"You're the second person to ask us that," Liam says. "What do you mean by *meet*?"

"What else would I say?" Spartacus shrugs. "I know you're innocent of whatever they're accusing you of. Most of us are."

The words hit Liam hard. How could so many men be locked up unfairly? "Titus is accused of trying to kill Caesar," he says.

"But I didn't!" Titus blurts out, his voice breaking. "I swear!"

"A murder accusation, no less? Someone must really hate you. And you?" he asks Liam.

"I guess I'm an accomplice. I was with Titus when they caught him. We were on our way to meet our friends when someone turned us in to the guards."

"You can still hope the Senate decides to investigate."

"I'm sure they will," Liam replies. "We've been falsely accused. They can't just throw us into the arena without a fair trial."

"If someone wants to use us as scapegoats, they'll find a way," Titus says. "That's what happened to my father. Evidence was planted against him, and the Senate decided his fate in less than an hour."

"And have you discovered who was behind it?" Spartacus asks. "I've always wondered."

"I thought it was Senator Septimus, but now I'm not sure. Still, I can't think of anyone else it could have been. He was friends with everyone."

Spartacus lets out a rough chuckle. "You are naïve if you believe there is friendship in the highest ranks of the Empire. The Senate is full of men willing to do anything they can to gain more power."

Titus stares at him, unblinking. "I remember being with my father in the Senate two days before his arrest and hearing some colleagues congratulate him on his future role as dictator. Maybe someone got jealous."

Spartacus winks at him. "You got your reason."

Liam recoils, wincing so hard his face twists. "Did you just say dictator? But a dictator is bad. Who would even want to be one?"

Titus looks genuinely stunned by the comment, which only confuses Liam more. "It's the highest magisterial position," Titus explains. "It gives extraordinary powers to a senator, but you need to be recommended by the Senate and approved by both consuls. There is nothing wrong with the role."

Liam softens. Maybe the word's meaning has

changed over the centuries. Where's Aria when you need her?

"After my father's arrest," Titus continues, "Septimus became dictator. It only added to my belief that it was him."

"I understand, but after what the forger gave us, I think we can rule him out," Liam says. "No one would fabricate something that could be used against them. It doesn't make sense."

"Nothing makes sense anymore," Titus replies.

"How did you end up here?" Liam asks Spartacus.

"I'm a Thracian. The Romans went to war against us, and I joined the fight against them. What we didn't know was that one of our own had betrayed us."

Liam and Titus lean forward to listen more closely to the story.

"We formed a special unit—twenty of the best warriors in our regiment. I was one of them. The plan was to launch a surprise attack at dawn. We were strong, smart, and better trained than anyone else in the region. But when we arrived, the Roman army was already waiting for us. Ten thousand soldiers led by a Roman senator."

Spartacus rises and moves to stand under the window, his back to the two boys as he gazes at the sky.

"One of our own sold us out," he goes on. "He worked for the Romans all along. The ambush wasn't created to win a battle; it was a trap to capture us alive. They wanted to use us as gladiators for the Romans' entertainment. Puppets."

His voice tightens as he says, "They brought us to Rome in chains. Since then, some of my brothers-in-arms have died in the arena."

Liam and Titus stay quiet. Nothing they can say would be the right thing. The moment feels sacred, like an invisible tribute to fallen warriors.

Liam dares to ask, "Is it really hard to fight in the arena?"

Spartacus frowns. "Yes. The lion won't show you mercy. It's either him or you. You'll get to choose one weapon, and that choice will mean the difference between life or death. But nothing to worry about for now. You might not have to participate in a match."

The word *match* sounds wrong. It's as if they're talking about a game, not a deadly conflict.

The door separating them from the rest of the jail opens. A Roman guard strides in and halts in front of the bars. He's holding a rolled parchment in his hand. He lifts and gives Liam and Titus a smirk.

"The Senate's decision is in. You'll fight tomorrow at noon, just in time for the lion's lunch."

FORTY

THE PUNISHMENT

Tiro glares at Gaia and Aria like they set fire to the school, or worse, the Senate.

Aria knows this look too well. It's the *I trusted you, and now I'm questioning every life decision I've ever made* face. Her dad's given it to Liam and her many times before.

Oliverus wears the grin of someone who thinks he's already won a secret battle that no one except him asked for. And from the corner, Septimus's mouth twitches with the same arrogant curve—father and son in perfect sync.

Tiro clears his throat. "Gaia, your mother and I work hard to give you the best chances in life. I even argued with her about you going to school so that you could learn to read and write. All I've ever wanted is for you to succeed."

He pauses. His voice is firm, but heavy with frustration as he continues, "Now I hear from my friend Septimus and his son that you left the house even though you are grounded to help the son of a criminal. And on top of that, a boy who tried to kill Caesar without mercy?"

"Father, Titus is not a criminal! He didn't try to kill Caesar!"

"You're defending him?" Tiro retorts. "I'm not used to punishing you, Gaia, but I don't have any choice now. You and Aria will stay in this house until further notice."

Aria feels herself unraveling. They don't have time for this. Liam and Titus are in danger. They can't be stuck here and leave their friends to die.

"Oliverus and I should go," Septimus says.

Tiro turns to his colleague. "Sorry you had to witness my daughter's outburst." He tilts his head at Oliverus. "Thank you for your help, Oliverus."

Aria's blood boils as she steps aside to let them pass. It takes everything in her not to lunge at Oliverus.

The door closes, and Gaia begins to speak. "Father, please listen to us. Someone did try to hurt Caesar, but it wasn't Titus. Another man went inside Septimus's office. I saw him with my own eyes."

"That's right," Aria says.

"Enough!" Tiro shouts. "You're only making things worse," he says, his voice like ice. "The Senate has made its decision. Titus and Liam were found guilty. As a punishment, they will fight in the arena tomorrow at noon for the opening games of the Quinquatria festival. You are not to intervene anymore. I can't let my daughter get dragged any deeper into this mess."

Aria feels as if the floor has opened beneath her, dropping her into the burning depths of the earth. *This can't be happening. Not Liam.* She forces herself to look at Tiro and says, "I swear to you, Mr. Carina, they're innocent. Liam was with Caius and me when Caesar was attacked in Septimus's office. He couldn't have done it. It wasn't them… It's Septimus! He's behind all of this."

Tiro leans back, and Aria sees how hard he's working not to explode. He draws in a long breath and says, "My wife likes you. It's the only reason I'm not throwing you out into the street. But once this matter is over, I'll have you sent back to Alexandria without your friend. Accusing a senator is serious, Aria. You should be grateful I don't have you arrested."

Aria blinks. She's unable to tell if she is dreaming or if this is reality. How can Tiro be so deaf?

Tiro calls for help. The guard who's usually posted in front of the villa enters, and Tiro orders him to take the girls to Gaia's bedroom. "Do not let them leave without my permission."

In a matter of minutes, Aria has gone from hopeful to desperate. On their way out of the office, a man in a light-colored tunic, too light to hide the dirt, passes them on his way into Tiro's office. His grin reveals crooked teeth, and the inflamed cut on his cheek only makes his whole creepy appearance even creepier.

The girls enter Gaia's bedroom. It might be comfortable, yet now it feels like a golden jail. A beautiful cage, but a cage all the same.

FORTY-ONE
THE WEAPON

Liam closes his eyes. His lips curl into a smile as he pictures a sunny field where all his friends are having a picnic. For a moment, he swears he can even smell grilled steak and baked potatoes.

"What are you thinking about?" Titus asks Liam, pulling him back to reality, back to the place he wishes he could escape from.

"Home."

"Dreaming about it won't change much."

"Maybe not," Liam says, smiling faintly. "But it keeps me going."

Spartacus's deep voice interrupts them. "You two can come train with me." One guard leads a few paces ahead, while another watches from behind.

"Thank you ... I guess," Titus whispers to Spartacus.

"But how did you convince them to let us train with you? They don't exactly seem like they want us to win."

"The crowd wants entertainment, and there won't be any if you get eaten in the first minute."

"That's so thoughtful," Liam replies through gritted teeth.

"Fighting is my job," Spartacus says. "And I will teach you everything I can to help you survive tomorrow."

Liam grimaces. He doesn't know about Titus, but he has far less faith in himself than Spartacus seems to.

"Can you help us choose a weapon?" Titus asks Spartacus.

"Yes, and you'll need to choose wisely. The good news is that if you win tomorrow, you'll be set free."

"Oh, fantastic news," Liam says with a laugh that's half-sarcasm.

They arrive at an open courtyard inside the jail grounds. Along the high walls that keep the prisoners inside, Roman Vigiles stand guard, their bodies weighed down by armor and swords, ready for any escape attempt. In the center, a muddy field serves as a training area, where several hardened gladiators clash in brutal combat.

Liam's shoulders tense. These men are at least twice his size, both in height and width. He glances down at his arms. They are so thin it's almost embarrassing. If he'd known this was coming, he might've gone to the gym back at school a few more times. But really, how could anyone have predicted they'd end up in a Roman arena?

And for once, it isn't even Aria's fault.

"Come on, boys," Spartacus calls, leading them to a rack along the one wall, stacked with every type of weapon Liam can imagine, and some he can't. Swords with gleaming blades, spears longer than his body, and tools so odd-looking he couldn't name them if he tried.

There are no embellishments on them; they're just cold, brutal steel and wood.

"Let's find you something to fight with," Spartacus says. "I know these weapons look intimidating, but we will find one you can handle."

Spartacus hands Liam a sword. It's not too scary. It's the same length as his arm, with a simple wooden handle that isn't too large, so his hand won't look out of proportion.

Liam picks it up with confidence.

For half a second.

Then its weight drags him to the ground like a sack of bricks.

"Ouch!" he cries as he tumbles into the dirt.

He lets go of the weapon. Spartacus offers him a helping hand, which Liam takes. He pulls himself up and leaves the sword where it landed.

"Well, I guess that one's not for me," Liam mutters, brushing the mud off his tunic.

"Let me try," Titus says, stepping forward with purpose.

He rubs his hands together, then grips the sword's handle and lifts it from the ground with a sharp motion. The force nearly throws him off-balance, but he recovers quickly.

"Wow, you're good," Liam says in awe. The ease with

which Titus swings the sword makes him feel weak. *Why can't I do that?*

"You're a natural," Spartacus says. "Looks like you've found your weapon, Titus. Go ahead and practice while Liam and I keep looking for something he can use."

Liam tries to stay upbeat, but it's not easy.

Spartacus turns back to the display of weapons, scanning the racks with laser focus. His finger trails along a row of sword hilts until it stops at another weapon, this one longer and thinner than the last, almost like a spear.

He grabs it and holds it out to Liam. "Try this one."

Liam wipes his sweaty palms on his tunic. With both hesitation and hope, he grips the hilt.

It doesn't feel too heavy. Encouraged, he holds it tighter and raises it high. When he gets the blade to shoulder height, the sword falls to the ground and starts to take Liam down with it. He lets go just in time to avoid crashing face-first into the mud again.

Liam gets up, leans over, hands resting against his knees, eyes locked on the ground.

If he can't even hold a weapon for more than a second, how is he supposed to fight a wild animal?

He holds his breath, willing the tears not to rise. All he hears in his head is one cruel, looping thought: *You're weak, and that weakness is going to get you killed.*

FORTY-TWO
A BOW AND ARROW

On the training field, Liam wipes a tear from the corner of his eye.

"Well," Spartacus says, picking up the latest sword they've tried off the ground, "swords might not be your thing."

"I'm just not as strong as you or Titus."

"It's not about strength."

"You're just saying that to make me feel better."

Spartacus points across the yard. "See that man over there? Would you say he lacks strength?"

Liam turns and squints. A mountain of a man lifts a boulder bigger than Titus and himself put together like it's made of feathers.

"He's a colossus!" Liam blurts, making Spartacus chuckle.

"He is. And yet, he's never been able to lift a single one of these swords."

"Wait, what?"

"These weapons aren't ordinary," Spartacus explains. "They're enchanted. The goddess Minerva assigns a weapon to each fighter." He nods at the strongman. "Achilles's gift is brute strength. That's why no sword accepts him. And for you, well, we just haven't found your match yet."

Liam's amazement shifts to skepticism. *Here we go again.*

Sure, his trip to Egypt showed him that gods *could* exist, but his scientific mind still refuses to accept that mythology might be more than just stories. And honestly, he doesn't have the energy to learn an entirely new pantheon right now.

I miss Aria, he thinks, sighing.

"You must have a natural talent for another weapon," Spartacus says. "Any ideas?"

"Uh … I'm not exactly used to being in these kinds of situations."

"Maybe wrestling? It's popular in Alexandria, right?"

"It's not really my thing, especially when the opponent is a lion. If I want to survive, I might be better off with a bow and arrow," Liam says, laughing nervously.

Spartacus claps his hands in triumph and darts to a nearby shack which, oddly enough, looks like the Santa Claus cabin set up at the end of Concordia Avenue in Sommetville at Christmas time.

When Spartacus returns with a bow and an arrow, a pulse of hope beats through Liam.

"Try these," Spartacus says as he hands Liam the objects.

"Wow," Liam exclaims as he takes both items with enthusiasm. Finally, something he can use that doesn't knock him over. He squares his shoulders and fits the arrow to the string.

With calm precision, he draws the string, takes aim at a hay-stuffed mannequin, and lets the arrow fly.

The arrow streaks through the air like a shooting star.

Liam allows himself a proud smile. At last, something he knows how to do well. But his smile vanishes when Achilles's scream echoes across the yard.

FORTY-THREE
VALERIAN

Aria paces back and forth in Gaia's bedroom. Like usual, being under a tight deadline helps her focus. Her thoughts get clearer with each step she takes across the marble floor. Staying calm under stress is a quality Liam has always admired in her, and she can't let him down.

"What are we going to do?" Gaia asks, her voice full of apprehension.

"I don't know yet, but I'll figure it out," Aria replies.

Seated at the edge of her bed, Gaia takes a pillow and presses it against her chest. "How can you not panic?"

Aria stops midstride and looks straight at her friend. "Worrying won't help, but doing something might. We're going to move forward with my plan to steal the guards' uniforms so we can get into the jail. And we have to act fast."

Gaia collapses backward onto her bed. "Fine, but how are we supposed to get out of here? My room is being guarded like a prison."

Aria looks out the window at the garden. One guard is stationed near the fountain at the center, and they can hear the guard on the other side of the door chewing loudly on mastic gum. Getting out without being seen seems almost impossible.

"The garden is probably the only way out," Gaia says. "We'd never make it through the front door."

Aria clutches the gold key hanging from her necklace. Her mother had given it to her on her fifth birthday, saying it would always carry her love inside it. Since then, Aria's never taken it off. It's her lucky charm—the source of the courage, optimism, and comfort she needs when things get hard. The smooth gold surface warms under her fingers, and memories of Egypt rush back to her.

"We can put them to sleep," she says.

Gaia's eyebrows knit together. "What?"

"We can put the guards and the rest of the house to sleep. We just need to find a plant like valerian. Then we mix it into their food or water and wait for it to work."

"You're serious?"

"Completely. It's safe."

"But where are we going to find something like that? I don't exactly keep sedatives in my room."

Aello leaps onto Gaia's bed with practiced ease. Gaia opens her arms, and the little dog snuggles in as she plants a kiss on her tiny forehead.

"Can Aello get it for us?" Aria asks.

Gaia's expression warms for the first time in hours. "That's a great idea. No one will think twice about her going outside. Everyone knows she needs to go out to pee."

Aria looks wistfully at Gaia and Aello together. She wishes she could have a bond like theirs with her own dog. "I've always said a dog is more than a pet. My father refuses to let me have one, but I'll try again once I get back home."

"You should! I can't imagine not having Aello with me," says Gaia. "Now, let's work on your plan."

She heads to her desk and pulls out a blank sheet of parchment. She scribbles a note, rolls it tightly, and ties it to Aello's collar.

"Go see our apothecary, girl," Gaia whispers. "The fate of Titus and Liam is in your paws."

Aello wags her tail and trots to the garden door. Aria

opens it and, with one last look at her mistress, she slips outside.

"Do you think the apothecary will give her what we need?" Aria asks.

"Yes. It's not the first time we've sent Aello to pick something up for us."

"Perfect. Now we wait." Aria sighs and sits on her bed. Waiting is not exactly her strong suit.

Gaia joins her. "Waiting here isn't easy, but at least we have a plan. That gives me hope. It's just every time I think about Titus, I feel like crying."

Aria puts an arm around her shoulders. "I know. I'm doing everything I can to not think about what will happen to Liam if we fail. I don't know what I'd do without him. But worrying won't change anything. We need to stay strong for them."

"I wish I were as brave as you."

Aria's smile barely has time to bloom before the bedroom door swings open.

FORTY-FOUR
THE ENEMY

Aria and Gaia turn to see Faustina, the maid, standing in the bedroom doorway.

"Dinner will be served soon," she says. "Your mother requests you both join her at the table. Mr. Caius will be dining with you."

"We're coming," Gaia replies.

When they enter the dining room, Aria looks around with curiosity. The furnishings don't resemble any dining room she's familiar with. There isn't a large table in the center. Instead, three low rectangular sofas form a U-shape, all facing two round tables big enough to hold a platter. The sofas don't have backrests but are covered with cushions and bolsters.

Caius is already there, seated on the sofa in the

middle. He stands when he sees them, smiling warmly with open arms. "I hear there's been some drama with your parents," he says while he hugs Gaia.

"News travels fast," Gaia says.

"There is no need to concern yourself with the situation," Caius tells her. "They're just upset. It'll pass. If my parents disowned me every time they got mad, I'd have been on my own by age seven! Let's forget the drama and enjoy dinner."

"You're probably right," Gaia mutters as her parents enter.

Gaia and Aria sit on the sofa with their backs to the door, across from her parents. Caius returns to his place in the center, positioned like a mediator.

Tiro begins a long-winded speech condemning the actions of Titus and Liam. Aria notices Gaia tense up beside her. She takes her hand and gives it a steady squeeze. Now isn't the time to react. They have to stay calm if they want their plan to work.

"Will you join us tomorrow for the dinner?" Tiro asks Caius.

"What dinner?" Gaia asks.

"We don't owe you an explanation," Tiro replies with a toughness Aria didn't realize he had in him. "But since you asked, we're hosting a gathering with the city's top senators."

"Will Septimus be here?" Aria asks.

"Yes," Caius says.

"And will Caesar come?" Gaia asks in turn.

"Yes," Caius says.

Aria grows more and more restless. Everything around her feels like it's moving too fast to take in. Could Septimus be planning to strike at tomorrow's gathering?

Faustina holds out a bronze platter shaped like a giant spoon to Aria. "Would you like some puls? It's one of Rome's specialties."

Aria isn't hungry. Worry has filled her so completely there's no room for food. She looks at the oatmeal-like food on the platter and is almost glad she doesn't want to eat. She hates oatmeal!

"No, thank you," she mumbles. Faustina moves on to Gaia, who also declines the food. Only the adults seem to have an appetite tonight.

Caius picks up an apple from a platter on the table and bites into it with gusto. "Tiro, are you still inviting Caesar after what happened this afternoon?"

Aria and Gaia side-eye each other.

"Of course I am," Tiro replies. "It was only a small incident."

"What happened exactly?" Marcia asks, tilting her head in curiosity.

Tiro fumbles with the piece of bread in his hand. "Nothing important. Caesar and I disagree on some policies regarding taxation."

"In what way?" Marcia asks.

"It would only bore you. Let's not dwell on it."

Marcia sets her spoon down on the table. "I might be a woman, but I am still a citizen of Rome, and I have the right to know what is happening politically. So, kindly answer me."

Tiro seems to stop breathing, and Aria has to hide her satisfaction. She never would have expected Marcia to speak up like this.

After swallowing his bread, Tiro finally says, "Caesar has proposed a plan that would raise taxes on senators while lowering them for other professions. I simply don't think it will benefit the country. If Caesar wants to become dictator, he needs to serve everyone, not just the poorest."

Marcia studies her husband for a few seconds, then calmly picks up her spoon and goes back to her soup.

Dinner ends soon after, and once they're allowed to leave, the girls rush back to their room.

Gaia flops onto her bed and stares at her ceiling. "I thought this dinner would never finish!"

Aria rolls her tongue along the insides of her teeth. It's a trick her teacher taught her a few years ago. It helps her take her time to think instead of blurting out something too harsh too quickly. She needs to discuss Tiro's argument with Caesar without hurting Gaia's feelings. "I'm just wondering if your father might now have a motive to kill Caesar." Not the best way to put it, but there aren't many ways to say something like that.

Gaia startles. "What? Are you mad? Are you saying this because of their argument?" She doesn't wait for Aria to answer and adds, "It took place *after* the attempt on Caesar's life, which shows my father has nothing to do with this. Plus, the man in Septimus's office wasn't working for him. I'm certain of it! I saw him with my own eyes."

"But how can you be certain? You said yourself he was wearing a hood so you couldn't see his face."

Gaia shakes her head so hard Aria worries for a second that it might snap off.

"No, no, no. My father has nothing to do with this. It's Septimus who is behind the plot."

"Can we be sure? We've been focused on Septimus from the start, but maybe we're wrong, and Liam's right. It's strange for someone as clever as him to leave behind so much evidence."

"Maybe that's the point. He left clues so big that no one would believe they're real."

Aria sits on Gaia's bed and covers her face. Maybe if she hides her eyes, this whole situation will vanish and she'll wake up back in Sommetville. Liam will be there, waiting for the perfect moment to tease her. She never thought she could miss someone this much.

She lowers her hands. No Liam, no Sommetville.

"Maybe you're right," she says. "So many facts are piling up, and I don't know who to trust anymore. I was just playing devil's advocate."

Gaia sighs. "It's okay. And perhaps ... perhaps we should go ask Caius for help tomorrow."

"Why? Do you think he'd take our side?"

"Yes. He's supported us from the start, and when I told him and my father what Titus overheard about the assassination attempt, he almost believed me. He was more convinced than my father, who refused to act."

Aria thinks for a moment. "It's true that back in Septimus's office, Caius barely hid his suspicion about

Septimus's involvement. So it might be easy to convince him. But what about my plan?"

"I'm sorry, but your plan… It's mad."

"What do you mean, mad?" Aria crosses her arms, feeling defensive.

"I mean, dressing up as guards? Knocking them out? It's suicidal!"

Aria softens her expression. Okay, maybe Gaia has a point. "All right. We'll find Caius tomorrow morning and try to convince him to help us release Liam and Titus. But are you sure Aello can get the valerian in time? We still need to be able to leave the house."

As if she knew they were talking about her, the sound of tiny paws on gravel drifts into the room. Aello steps inside, one paw at a time, her little head held high. She climbs onto a stool beside her mistress's bed and jumps onto a pillow resting on the cover.

"Aello, here you are! Just in time to prove to Aria how smart you are." Gaia drops a kiss on her dog's forehead.

"You sure did. And did you bring the valerian?" Aria asks Aello.

Gaia unties a small vial from Aello's collar and holds it up. "Looks like it. Though it's not a lot."

"How many people live in this house again?" Aria

asks. She's still trying to keep track of all the guards and servants swarming the place.

"Around twenty, I think."

"Then it's enough. Valerian is powerful. I promise that by lunchtime tomorrow, this house will be so quiet, it'll be like no one lives here."

Gaia laughs, and the tension lifts for a moment. They climb into bed and try to rest, but the only thought dominating Aria's mind is the fact they have less than twenty-four hours left to save their friends.

FORTY-FIVE
THE CULPRIT

Liam and Titus collapse onto their mattresses, but the damp and mud have seeped into them, spoiling the cell's only touch of comfort. Liam doesn't even care that he's now covered in grime. At this point, he just wants to lie down.

The training session drained them more than they expected and almost ended in disaster. Liam nearly pierced Achilles's ankle with an arrow. Liam shot his arrow so quickly that the gladiator didn't see it and walked across the line of fire. He let out a startled yell but thankfully wasn't hurt.

At least now that the training session has ended, Liam feels more confident. Titus and he aren't ready to face a lion, not by a long shot, but they have a sliver of hope. And Liam, deep down, still believes Aria will save them before they ever see the inside of the arena.

"I think dinner's coming soon," Spartacus says, settling onto his bench just as a guard locks them into their cell. "There's nothing like a good meal to help you recover."

"A *good* meal? That's optimistic," Liam says.

"You think they let us starve? A bunch of weak gladiators wouldn't make for a very entertaining fight."

Just minutes later, a guard comes carrying a tray with a steaming bowl of barley and a generous plate of roasted meat. He slides it through the slot at the bottom of the door.

Liam pouts. One tray. That's it?

"They must've forgotten yours," Spartacus says. He calls out to the guard. "Hey, they didn't get theirs."

"Fine. We'll bring something," the guard grumbles.

He comes back with another tray and pushes it into the cell. Liam jumps to grab it but stops cold when he sees what's on it. Two dry pieces of bread and a single glass of water.

Titus peers over Liam's shoulder. "What's wrong?"

"Looks like we're not on the VIP meal plan."

"Don't take it personally," Spartacus says. "You can take the rest of my food. I've eaten enough."

They thank him and wolf down the last of Spartacus's meal.

"Can you describe the man who attacked Caesar?" Spartacus asks.

"He wore a hood, but I caught a glimpse of his face," says Titus. "I'm sure he was Gallic, and definitely a slave because I saw the metal collar around his neck through an opening in the cape. He was maybe twenty, average height, thin, like he hasn't eaten enough. He had a scar on his right cheek."

Spartacus rubs his chin. "Septimus did launch a campaign in Gaul about a decade ago. I'm sure he brought back some men as slaves; that's what the Romans do. Still, I can't say if the slave who attacked Caesar belongs to Septimus."

"My father wasn't friends with Septimus, so I never went to his house," Titus says. "I won't recognize any of his staff."

Titus and Spartacus both turn to Liam, waiting for his opinion.

"Don't look at me like that," Liam says. "I have no idea. I'm still trying to wrap my head around the fact that slavery even exists."

"Let's just pray Gaia and Aria find a way to save us," Titus says.

"Who are they? Some friends of yours?" Spartacus asks, and the boys answer with quick yeses.

Spartacus goes still, deep in thought. Something in his expression shifts.

"What?" Liam questions.

"Nothing…" Spartacus hesitates.

"Come on. Tell us," Titus insists.

Spartacus leans in. "If someone is willing to send two innocent boys to their death just to stay hidden, they won't stop until every witness is gone. If they learn you have friends trying to prove your innocence, the real culprit will want to silence them too. Are you sure your enemies don't know about the girls?"

Liam feels like he has just been hit with a brick. Until now, he hadn't thought of that possibility. He clutches his head, his thoughts whirling like a tornado. He's only been thinking about himself, hoping Aria would find a way to get them out. But what if *she's* in even more danger?"

The color leaves Titus's face, as if this new fear has taken everything from him. "It's my fault. You came to rescue me, and now all our lives are at risk."

Liam grips Titus's shoulders and looks him straight in the eyes. "Hey, stop saying that. I came willingly and I'd do it again. We'll make it out and finish what we started. Don't give up. Now let's get some sleep so we can kick that lion's ass tomorrow."

Titus's lips curl into the hint of a smile, and he nods. Liam lets go and returns to his mattress. He lies down, rolling so his back faces Titus. His true feelings are now plastered across his face. His hope melts away faster than a burning candlestick, and he can't let Titus see it happen.

Only one thing is clear: He has to survive the arena. Not just to save himself, but to save Aria.

FORTY-SIX
FRIENDS

Septimus watches his slave light the oil lamp outside through his office window. Night has just fallen, and soon it will be time for dinner. He needs a good one to refuel his energy.

Someone knocks on the door, and Septimus orders them to enter. Oliverus peeks his head in, and he lets a few seconds pass before approaching his father's desk with a parchment in his hand.

"Look, Father, I got an A on my reading test," he says with a smile spreading all the way to his ears.

Septimus fixes him with a glare that drains the joy from Oliverus's face.

"Do you really think I care about your exam?" Septimus says. "There is a murderer at large, and you interrupt me with this nonsense?"

Oliverus's stomach drops. "I thought … I thought everything was under control. You said…"

"Politics isn't a children's game. And I'm beginning to doubt you have the intellect to ever sit beside me in the Senate."

He turns back to the window. "Leave. And do not bother me again tonight."

Oliverus flees the room before his father can see the tears welling in his eyes.

He truly believed his father would be proud, for once. But not even getting good grades works.

A heavy, aching loneliness takes root in his heart. It spreads as he walks to his room, where the calm feels colder than usual.

He wishes he had someone, anyone, to talk to. But at school, no one speaks to him. He's driven everyone away with his mean comments, bullying, and constant need for attention. He thought that if he acted like his father, he would earn the same respect. But it didn't work, and each day became harder than the last. He used to feel powerful after picking on someone; now he does it out of habit, and the disgust and shame he feels are slowly eating him alive.

His thoughts drift to Gaia and her friends. He would never admit it aloud, but he envies them. Gaia has everything he longs for—a warm family, real friends, people who care.

Curling up on his bed, he pulls the blanket over his head. The jealousy and sadness gripping him weigh more than any Roman armor.

FORTY-SEVEN
THE HOT CHOCOLATE

With her eyes closed, Aria feels something soft tickling on her cheek. She cracks one eyelid open, only to be blinded by a ray of sunlight. "Is it morning?" she mumbles. Aello barks, jolting her fully awake. "What is it? What's happening?" Aria's brow furrows, and she recoils when she finds Aello's rear far too close to her face for comfort.

From her bed, Gaia says, "Aello is just waking you up. She loves tickling guests with her tail."

"It's even better than an alarm clock."

Gaia gives her a puzzled look. Right, alarm clocks probably aren't a thing in ancient Rome. Aria decides there's no time to explain modern inventions. She has more important things to do this morning, like making twenty people fall asleep.

Gaia walks over to her wardrobe and pulls out a dress. "So how exactly are we going to get everyone to drink the valerian? I don't see the guards volunteering."

Aria grins. "Simple. I'll make one of my favorite drinks, hot chocolate, and introduce it as a very special beverage with powers they won't be able to resist."

"Hot what?"

Aria gasps. "You not knowing about hot chocolate might be a bigger crime than anything else we're doing."

Gaia giggles.

"There's no time to explain. You won't get to taste it now, but I'll give you the recipe later. Where's the kitchen?" Aria looks for her shoes.

"In the cave downstairs, but I never go there. Why would I?"

"To get a snack?" Aria says, then realizes Faustina would probably be the one sent to fetch anything Gaia wants to eat. "Let's get back to the plan. I'll go see your mother and say I want to prepare a special treat for her, as an apology for lying."

"Okay, but she might ask for the recipe and let the cook make it. Why would you do it instead of the person hired for that purpose?" Gaia asks, as if the idea of doing anything herself were unthinkable.

Aria pauses, then brightens. "I know! I'll say it's a

secret Egyptian recipe with miraculous anti-aging powers, something only I can make, for privacy purposes."

Gaia snorts. "You really do know her. She'd drink a whole bucket of it if she thinks it can remove her wrinkles."

"Let's hope you're right."

When they open the bedroom door, they find the guard snoring on the floor. It's one less person to deal with.

Aria leads the way toward the atrium, where Gaia's mother seems to spend most of her time when she's not entertaining.

"Mrs. Carina," Aria calls out while Gaia stays in the doorway.

Marcia lifts herself up until she is seated on the divan. "Aria? What can I do for you?"

"I just wanted to say how sorry I am for lying to you yesterday. I feel so bad. You welcomed Liam and me with open arms, and you didn't deserve it."

"I most definitely did not."

"And to make up for it, I'd like to share a special drink only known by Alexandrians with you. It'll wake up your taste buds and help you look even younger than you already do."

A flicker of excitement crosses Marcia's face before she swiftly masks it.

"I know it can't make up for our actions," Aria adds, "but I thought you could maybe introduce it to the Roman elite. Believe me, they'll sing your praises once they see the results."

Marcia clears her throat, trying to sound indifferent. "Are you saying this drink has anti-aging properties?"

"How do you think Egyptian women always look ten years younger than they really are?" Aria winks.

A silence stretches between them. Aria holds her breath until Marcia finally says, "What you did was serious, but I will take you up on your offer. Just know this won't change your punishment. You and Gaia are still grounded."

"I don't expect anything in return, Mrs. Carina. I just need your authorization to use your kitchen."

"You have it. I'll be waiting here. And don't forget to teach the cook the recipe."

"I won't," Aria says, already rushing off. Gaia shows her the way to the stairs leading to the underground kitchen. The door is hidden behind the paintings covering the wall. It is so well concealed that Aria would never have guessed it was there.

"You do know she's already planning a party to debut your 'miracle' drink, right?" Gaia says.

"By the time they realize it doesn't do anything, I'll be long gone."

Both girls burst into laughter and bound down the stairs two at a time to the kitchen.

FORTY-EIGHT

THE WAKE-UP CALL

Mogurix wakes with something wet and slimy licking his face. He blinks open one eye and stares straight into the huge nostrils of a donkey.

For a second, he thinks he must be dreaming. But the donkey's loud braying shatters the illusion.

"What in the world?" he groans.

The shock sends him scrambling to his feet with a yelp, which spooks the animal. The donkey breaks into a clumsy trot and lumbers out of the stable where Mogurix sleeps.

The sun is already high in the sky. Mogurix taps his forehead and sighs. He's overslept, another mistake.

Last night, he stayed up too long, dreading his master's order to kill the two girls.

He shakes the hay from his sandals. He never takes them off, just in case his master calls for him.

He leaves the stable to embark on his deadly mission. First Gaia and Aria. Then the forger.

FORTY-NINE
THE CONSPIRACY

Liam lies on his mattress and watches the first rays of sunrise crawl across the sky through the tiny window. He hasn't slept much. Trying to untangle who truly tried to kill Caesar has kept him awake. The good thing? His mind has been too busy to dwell on the arena.

He can't shake the uneasy feeling that he might be wrong about Septimus. Maybe Aria was right all along. Septimus has a motive. Caesar could have discovered Septimus was behind the scam, and now the latter wants to silence him.

From the mattress beside him, Titus taps him lightly on the arm. "Hey, Liam. Did you get any sleep?"

"No. I couldn't. With everything that's happened, and this rock-hard mattress, it's hard to get any good rest."

"I get that. But honestly, I don't think the sleeping arrangement is too bad."

Liam raises an eyebrow. "Excuse me?"

"At least we've got a straw mattress. It's better than what I sleep on these days. Which is the floor."

"You're serious?"

A loud snore from Spartacus cuts through the cell, and both boys hold their breath for a second, hoping not to wake the gladiator.

Liam blinks in disbelief. Sleeping on the floor? He suddenly feels very privileged when he thinks of his life back home. He wouldn't last a week in Titus's shoes. "I'm really sorry to hear that. You don't deserve it."

"Nobody does. But it's okay. I'm used to it." Titus shrugs. "In a few hours, it won't matter anymore. I will be asleep forever."

"Look, we'll be fine," Liam replies, though his voice is a half note higher than usual. "You're good with a sword. I'm decent with a bow. And once we get through this mess, we'll stop the person behind all of it."

"Yeah, but apart from Septimus, I really don't know who it could be. Gaia and I focused on him because all the clues pointed in his direction."

"I know. And now I'm starting to wonder if Septimus really is guilty."

"Are you serious?" Titus blurts, his voice too high. Liam quickly shushes him.

They hold still for a moment, waiting to see if Spartacus stirs. When he doesn't, Titus goes on. "You saw the forger's note, the one saying Septimus confessed. You were right. Why would he accuse himself of murder? And why wouldn't he just write the note himself in this case?"

Liam says, "To make sure he is never found guilty. It's actually pretty clever. Once Caesar is dead and he's accused due to the amount of proof against him, he calls for an investigation. They find the forger, and bam, he looks innocent. The forger only saw the senator's slave, so all Septimus has to do is get rid of his man, and he's safe."

"Okay, but kill another person?" asks Titus.

Liam side-eyes Titus. "I don't think he cares anymore."

"I guess you're right…"

"Or…" Liam holds up a finger. "Septimus is innocent, and it's Tiro or Caius who are behind the plot."

Titus's face twists in horror. "Tiro? How can you even say that? While you are at it, why don't you accuse Caesar of plotting his own murder?"

Liam tilts his head, Titus's last words replaying in his

mind. "Actually … maybe. Maybe Caesar did this to try to frame someone."

"You're losing your mind."

"Perhaps. When it comes to Tiro, Gaia told him about overhearing the plot to kill Caesar, and two days later guards were chasing her. It could be a coincidence … but I doubt it."

"Are you saying he would harm his own daughter to cover his crimes?"

"Based on what I've seen during my time here, I believe anyone is capable of just about anything in this city. Honestly, people seem a little crazy in this era. And Tiro could be behind the scam; remember, he wasn't blackmailed."

"Not true. He was."

"Really? Gaia didn't tell us that. Why was he blackmailed?"

"She's too embarrassed to say. And I'd rather not spread the reason any farther."

"That's nice. You're a good friend," Liam says. "What about Caius? Do you think he could be behind it?"

Titus exhales. "If he was guilty, why would he invite you and Aria to the Senate on the very day his man was planning to commit murder?"

"So he could have an alibi."

"Okay, but he was scammed by the blackmailer as well. When the secret of his affair came out during my father's trial—the very secret he was being blackmailed for—his wife left him. He lost more than money."

"It leads back to Septimus as the only option."

The door to their section opens, and footsteps pound toward them. Liam and Titus stand up.

Two guards stop in front of their cell. One of them grins. "Time to die, boys."

The key turns in the lock with a sharp click. Spartacus jolts awake. In a split second, he is on his feet. He meets Liam's and Titus's scared gazes and gives them each a pat on the back.

The guards step inside and slap thick iron cuffs on the boys' wrists. Liam bites his lower lip to keep from complaining as the cold metal digs into his skin.

As they leave their cell, Liam hears Titus's heart pounding in the same frantic rhythm as his own.

The moment they've dreaded is here.

FIFTY
ROMAN POLITICS

The Carina villa has been plunged into silence. Convincing the household to drink the hot chocolate was surprisingly easy. The rich aroma alone tempted most people, but when Aria told them the drink was a rare Egyptian elixir of youth, no one resisted. After all, no one wants to get old.

Some of the staff seemed to really love the sugary drink from the first sip and even asked for second servings. Aria just hopes the valerian was strong enough to knock them out but not cause other side effects like coma or worse, death. If that happens, she'll have a bigger problem on her hands.

Except for Tiro, who had left early for his office at the Senate, the entire household now sleeps soundly. Which means she and Gaia can finally make their move.

With Aello beside them, Aria and Gaia slip out the front door and take the direction of Caius's house, only a few blocks away. When they arrive, panting, Gaia pounds on the door with both fists.

Caius's sister, who has been living with him since his divorce, greets them in the vestibule with a surprised expression. "Gaia? What are you—?"

"Is Caius here?" Gaia interrupts. "We need to speak with him. It's urgent."

"He's already left for the Colosseum," she replies. "Septimus isn't feeling well, so Caius is managing the games in his place."

Aria feels dizzy. She doesn't think she has the strength to handle another problem today. Caius was her last hope for saving Liam and Titus. Because, as painful as it is to admit, her plan is dangerous and carries a high risk of failure.

Back on the street, Gaia says, "We need to go to the Colosseum."

"What does 'manage the games' mean?" Aria asks her friend.

"It's tradition," Gaia explains. "A dictator—a senator with extraordinary powers—presides over the games and decides who lives and who dies. Septimus is the only dictator in the Empire right now. That's why he's so powerful."

Aria groans and presses her fingers to her temples. "Right, the Senate hierarchy. But why ask Caius to stand in for him? Why not your father?"

"Normally, Caesar would take Septimus's place, as he is the next senator in line to become dictator. But after the attack, he probably doesn't feel safe, or he is sick, I don't know. And Caius is next in line after Caesar."

Aria's mind spins. Roman politics are more complicated than any logic puzzle she's ever tried to solve.

"So that's the motive!" she barks. "Septimus doesn't want another senator to become dictator because it would diminish his power. Caesar is close to getting the status, so Septimus decides to get rid of the competition."

Gaia hurries to match Aria's pace. "That's exactly the conclusion Titus and I reached," says Gaia. "His father was set to become dictator but after what happened to him, the title went to Septimus."

"Every piece fits!" Aria says, then shivers as a new thought spreads through her mind like wildfire. "But if Septimus is framing Liam and Titus, why would he give up control of the games? Why would he let someone else decide their fate and risk them winning and speaking out against him?"

"Maybe he's so sick he can't move. Look on the bright side: With Caius in charge, he might spare Liam and Titus."

For a moment, hope returns and Aria smiles. But the thought quickly crashes against a rising wave of fear. What if Septimus *isn't* guilty? What if she's wrong?

Two feelings twist inside her. Optimism and dread tangle like vines until she can barely breathe.

FIFTY-ONE

THE CHASE

Mogurix climbs the low stone ledge to peek over the wall of the Carinas' estate, only to blink in disbelief. The guards are sprawled across the lawn, fast asleep. Not a soul stirs.

He drops back down to the ground with a rising sensation of anxiety. The girls must be gone already. *I am too late.* His master will be so disappointed if he finds out Mogurix has let them slip through his fingers.

There's only one place they'd go: the Colosseum. That's where the boys are. He sets off at a fast pace, nervousness pushing his physical abilities.

He's hurrying down the main avenue leading to the arena when he spots a small white blur bouncing down the street. This is Aello. *What will happen to her once her mistress is gone?* Mogurix wonders, before shoving the thought as far away as he can. Gaia walks beside her dog.

He stays behind a group of women, who provide him with the perfect cover, until they reach the broad square in front of the Colosseum. The chase grows more difficult as the crowd thickens. Spectators press in from all sides.

He tries to keep up with the two girls, but a firm hand grabs his shoulder and drags him into some bushes. He finds himself in the strip of greenery at the center of the square, a place dotted with benches, fountains, statues, and trees.

His heart skips a beat when he discovers who's captured him. His master's face is red with rage, his jaw clenched like a trap about to snap.

FIFTY-TWO

THE CONVERSATION

Oliverus trails behind his mother as they head to the Colosseum. Despite her husband not feeling well, she insisted on attending the games.

"It's going to be spectacular," she told Oliverus at breakfast. "It would be a shame to miss it."

But Oliverus doesn't share her enthusiasm. He's still unsettled by everything that happened yesterday. He doesn't believe his father's sudden illness for a second. Septimus has never shown weakness in his life.

Oliverus is convinced his father is working on something, like putting the final touches on his plan to bring down Gaia's family. There's an important dinner scheduled for tonight, and knowing his father's flair for drama, Oliverus is certain he's preparing a grand finale worthy of one of Seneca's best tragedies.

As the crowd thickens around them, the distance between Oliverus and his mother grows. Eventually, he loses sight of her in the sea of people rushing for the entrances. He stops in the small garden facing the Colosseum, hoping to get a moment for himself. His excitement at watching Liam and Titus get torn apart by a lion has vanished. He doesn't even want to pretend to enjoy it anymore.

He sits on a bench and watches the jubilant masses stream by. Maybe he'll wait here until it's all over and find his mother afterward. In any case, there's little chance she'll notice his absence, let alone worry about him. That would be a first.

A sound behind him breaks his thoughts. Two men are speaking in low, urgent voices. Curiosity takes hold of him, and he strains to listen more closely.

"I'm sorry, Master… I swear I did everything I could to catch those two girls, but I lost them in the crowd," one man says in a trembling voice.

"You clearly didn't do enough," snaps the other voice. "Gaia and Aria are on the loose, and dangerously close to ruining everything. You're just a useless waste of coin."

"I am so sorry, Master."

"Now kill the two girls before the dinner tonight and go wait for me outside the house when you are done. We will get rid of Caesar tonight."

The man's voice is so cold and cruel that Oliverus wishes he could vanish into thin air. There's a short pause before the other man responds.

"Yes, Master," the first man mumbles, so quietly Oliverus almost doesn't hear it.

And with those last words, everything falls silent again.

Oliverus's heart quickens as the moment sinks in. The voices were unfamiliar, but the message was crystal clear: Caesar is going to be assassinated tonight, and Aria and Gaia are too. So many lives on the line.

Why are Aria and Gaia being targeted? What threat could they possibly pose to grown men scheming in the shadows?

He wants to run home and tell his father immediately, but a voice in his head tells him not to.

Would he even believe me?

His father rarely listens to him and never gives praise, instead always finding fault. There's every chance he'll brush Oliverus off.

But this isn't about pride. This is about lives.

I can't just do nothing. I am not a coward.

The sight of a fluffy white animal darting through the crowd flooding the Colosseum's entrance catches his eye. It's Aello. His eyes follow the dog, and sure enough, he sees Gaia walking alongside, her golden hair shining under the midday sun.

Should he warn her? She'd probably ignore him, or worse, think it's some kind of trap.

But then he steels himself. *Even if she hates me, she has to know.* This isn't some silly school game anymore. He's made bad choices for far too long. He used to think acting like his father would make him strong, but it only made him cruel. His father may never change, but he can. He's old enough to know what's right, and he'll prove it.

He gathers his courage, steps out of hiding, and runs toward her.

This time, I have to do the right thing.

THE GAME

Liam feels as if he's no longer in control of his own body. His legs seem to move on their own as they carry him down the prison corridor toward the Colosseum.

As Liam and Titus advance, more gladiators join the procession. Some of them he would have called muscular before coming here, but now they seem small as they stand with other men so massive they seem more monster than human.

"We can already guess who's going to end up as lion food," Liam mutters to Titus, who walks beside him.

"Shut up!" barks one of the guards. He raises the tip of his knife to threaten Liam.

Spartacus, who walks just ahead of Liam, glances back at him with a warning look. *This is not the time to draw attention.* Liam's mouth goes dry. Sarcasm is how he copes with fear, but right now it's not appropriate.

The prison gate opens to the route connecting to the Colosseum. A shaft of sunlight bursts across their path, momentarily blinding the group. They hear the crowd's chants rising from the Colosseum's open roof like a tidal wave.

Titus casts a terrified glance at Liam as the distance between them and the arena shrinks. But Liam still clings to one fragile hope: Aria will come.

Just as he reaches the gladiator's entrance into the Colosseum, he feels a presence. He glances to his right, and there she is.

Aria.

Running toward them.

Even from a distance, he sees the tears streaking her face.

FIFTY-FOUR
THE ARENA

Aria's tears blur her vision. Seeing Liam in chains has shaken her to her core. This isn't a game. The harshness of reality hits her like a meteorite. *What if Liam doesn't survive?*

Until now, some part of her had refused to believe he could die. The memories they've shared over the years swirl in her head, a bittersweet montage of friendship, love, and happiness.

"Aria, we need to go to the commoners' bleachers," Gaia says, shaking her out of her trance. "I think I just saw my dad go into the aristocrats' section. We can't be seen. Come on!"

Snapping back to the situation at hand, Aria follows Gaia toward the spectators' gate, the closest one to the gladiators' entrance where Liam entered a few seconds ago.

The crowd rushes in around them, pushing and shoving in a frenzy that reminds her of a concert. The excitement on their faces makes her sick.

Gaia and she squeeze through the mass of people and into a shadowy corridor below the stands. The spectators already seated above stomp their feet in a thunderous rhythm, excited for the violence to begin. Bits of dust and debris fall on their heads.

Battered by countless elbows, they finally reach an opening where a staircase leads up to the highest seats of the arena. They follow the crowd in and find two seats as more people pour inside.

Aria takes in the full scene in front of her, and her jaw drops open. The Colosseum is massive. Its oval shape looms below them, packed with thousands of spectators. The sand lies undisturbed in the center of the arena, waiting to be stained by the blood of honest men. The crowd buzzes in anticipation of what they call entertainment but is really just battle and murder.

Aria watches in disgust as nearby spectators snack on olives and figs, just like Liam and she used to do with popcorn at the movies. How can anyone enjoy this? It's history's darkest side.

She glances at Gaia, whose hand moves nervously

through Aello's fur. The dog lies curled in her lap, bouncing faintly with the tremble in Gaia's legs.

Oliverus has lost sight of Aria and Gaia in front of the Colosseum. A surge of people crowds in front of him, forcing him to slow down. With a dozen entrances and thousands of spectators, how will he ever find them? The task feels impossible.

As he weighs his options, the square outside the Colosseum begins to quiet. The last spectators make their way inside, and soon, the place is nearly deserted. A strident trumpet blast rings from within the amphitheater, signaling the start of the games.

He moves to the center of the square where he can watch several entrances. Searching for the girls inside the Colosseum is pointless. It's way too big. Plus, whatever happens to the two boys is out of his hands. All he can do is hope to save Aria and Gaia. That much, at least, is still possible.

And truthfully, he has no wish to see Liam and Titus devoured in front of thousands of onlookers.

Overcome with guilt, Oliverus lowers his head and

sobs. The weight of remorse presses down harder with every breath *he* gets to breathe.

FIFTY-FIVE
THE GATE OF DEATH

For a moment, Liam feels like he's back at his favorite summer fair. With his eyes closed, he pictures Aria, so excited she's bouncing on her toes like a kangaroo as she hands him a cotton candy. His friend Noah taps him on the shoulder, urging him toward the scene, where everyone is screaming in joy, clapping, buzzing with energy, ready to listen to their favorite band.

The same cheerful sounds resonate now, but this isn't a concert.

Liam, Titus, and the rest of the gladiators wait behind the Gate of Death, the barrier between them and the arena. The name isn't Liam's invention; he learned from Spartacus that's what it's really called.

The humidity in the holding room clings to Liam's skin and adds to the already thick layer of sweat on his body. The crowd's cheers rumble in his ears. He pinches his arm one last time, but nothing changes. He doesn't wake up. This is real, and he's moments away from meeting his fate.

"I feel like a rock star," he whispers sarcastically to Titus.

His companion gives Liam the tightest smile he has ever seen in his life. Titus must be too scared to banter back. Not everyone copes the same way in times of crisis.

A blast of trumpets makes his heart skip a beat.

"Psst." Spartacus leans in from behind them. "Remember, nothing is lost. You must join forces and fight together. The god of war, Mars, knows the truth of your innocence, and he'll watch over you."

Liam has never wanted to believe in the gods more than he does now. *This is not the moment to fail*, he tells himself, picturing Aria's face. And then he sees the face of his mother, his father, his sister, and everyone he loves in Sommetville.

A memory flares to life. Years ago, his mother offered him a plastic sword and shield after he became obsessed with a cartoon about Spartacus and the gladiators of Rome. He was so happy about his new gift that he sprinted to Aria's house, boasting he'd be the greatest gladiator ever.

"I'd like to see that," Aria said. "I bet you'd pee your-self if you were in a real arena with lions!"

Liam grins. Once again, she was wrong. He has not peed himself.

And he can't die before gloating to her about it.

A powerful surge of energy flows through him. He raises his chin and looks straight ahead.

A guard shouts behind them, and another one by the gate tugs at a rope hanging near the wall. With each pull, the metal gate groans upward, letting in the cheers of the thirsty crowd at full volume.

"You're the appetizers," the guard sneers, shoving Liam and Titus forward. "The lion doesn't like a heavy breakfast."

Liam's gaze lands on a cage at the far end of the arena. Thick iron bars create shadows over the animal inside, but not enough to hide its hulking frame. Its tawny coat gleams, and its mane flares like rays of the sun. Dark, unblinking eyes watch them with a chilling stillness. The lion is a reflection of the arena itself: grand, wild, and terrifying.

The guard shoves Liam forward. He stumbles, almost falls, but steadies himself just in time. He won't let anyone pile more disrespect on top of what he's already endured. Lifting his head, Liam walks into the arena on his own with Titus by his side.

His jaw slackens as he takes in the full size of the Colosseum. It's far more immense than he imagined. The crowd erupts into boos and taunts, turning the surreal moment into something grotesquely real.

In front of him, a grandstand shaded by a large piece of canvas takes center stage. On a gilded seat draped in red velvet cushions sits a familiar figure. Liam gasps as he watches Caius greet the crowds. Tiro is beside him, waving enthusiastically as well. Tiro leans toward Caius's ear, his lips moving in a whisper. Caius gives a small nod, and Tiro settles back in his seat. No sign of Septimus.

Last night, Spartacus explained the dictator's role during the games—he has the power to spare someone's life or sentence them to death. Seeing Caius gives Liam hope. Maybe he'll have mercy on Titus and him.

The guards remove the metal cuffs from the boys' wrists. His arms feel feather-light, though red welts remain. Liam and Titus try to shake off the sting as the gate slams shut behind them. They're alone now in front of bloodthirsty Roman spectators and a bloodthirsty predator.

Caius rises from his throne, his crimson cape fluttering in the breeze. He raises his hands and the musicians stop playing.

"People of Rome!" he booms. "Today, we honor Minerva, the goddess of wisdom and war. And what better way to start the game than with the punishment of two criminals!"

The crowd explodes in cheers. Liam grimaces, unsure of what he heard. Did Caius say *criminals*?

"These boys will face our most dangerous opponent, the lion," Caius continues in a strong voice. "To defend themselves, each may choose one weapon. That is the law. Let Spartacus, Rome's noblest gladiator, bring them their arms."

Spartacus steps into the arena and when his sandals stir the sand, they create swirling clouds. The spectators stomp their feet and clap. They chant his name so loudly that it creates tremors.

Spartacus walks with quiet authority, a sword in one hand, a bow and arrow in the other. He gives Titus the sword and Liam the bow and arrow. With the flair of a showman, he waves to the crowd like he is a god in human form.

"Let the game begin!" Caius says, his voice carrying over the noise.

A wave of cheers ripples through the arena until a bone-chilling growl splits the air. The revelers go quiet.

Liam's blood turns to ice.

A guard standing on top of the lion's cage yanks a

lever. At lightning speed, the gate swings open. The animal emerges from the dark like a phantom.

The lion prowls into the arena. It walks with the confidence of a creature who knows it's the king of all living beings.

It stops and surveys the entire area before locking eyes with Liam and Titus, daring them to move.

Liam puts his single arrow into the bow. His fingers tremble, slick with dampness, and he can barely grip the bow. The fear of dying collides with the fear of harming the lion. Liam feels trapped in a no-win situation: it's either his life or the animal's.

The lion opens its mouth and lets out a roar that reveals its deadly canines. The ground seems to shudder. Titus takes an instinctive step back. So does Liam.

As the creature takes a few paces forward, Liam raises his bow and fires.

The arrow whistles through the air. The crowd holds its breath.

A gust of wind whips up a flurry of sand, wrapping the lion in a dusty cloud. In an instant, it vanishes from view.

When the haze clears, the animal is still standing, uninjured but furious. The arrow is embedded in the ground just beside its front left leg.

The lion paws at the sand with savage impatience. Then it charges with rage in its muscles and murder in its eyes.

FIFTY-SIX
THE ATTACK

The enraged lion picks up speed and charges at Liam and Titus.

"Let's split up!" Liam shouts as loud as he can so Titus will hear him over the thudding of the lion's paws hitting the ground.

Liam and Titus take off in opposite directions. The lion hesitates, thrown off by their sudden movement. The extra second buys Liam just enough time to look for his arrow. He catches sight of the blade's silver gleam in the sand and runs to retrieve it.

But before he can get to it, he hears a cry of pain from the other side of the arena.

He turns to see Titus lying on the ground, gripping his right knee. Blood mixed with sand streaks down his leg from two long scratches. The scent has caught the lion's attention, and it heads for the fallen boy, who's struggling to rise.

The lion takes its time closing in on Titus, as if savoring the slow approach.

Deadly pressure begins to build inside Liam's chest. This is the type of decision that can mean life or death. He has his bow but no arrow. Does he go help Titus without a weapon, or try to grab his arrow first but risk being too late?

When the lion bares its fangs at Titus, Liam makes his choice. He races to his friend at a speed he didn't know he was capable of.

In one motion, he leaps, pushing off the earth with his right leg and landing on the lion's back. The animal growls in rage, twisting and thrashing to shake him off.

"Get up, Titus! You can do it!" Liam yells, clinging to the animal's mane.

Titus pushes himself up and limps toward his fallen sword. He picks it up and lifts his gaze just in time to see Liam slam to the ground, the lion's mouth closing around him.

FIFTY-SEVEN
THE HELMET

Aria covers her eyes and holds her breath, as if she can make time pause.

"This boy might be a criminal, but we can't deny his courage," says the woman seated next to her.

Aria drops her hands. What was Liam thinking, jumping onto the back of a lion at least ten times his weight, unarmed? Now he's sprawled on the ground, completely at the mercy of the animal.

She doesn't know exactly how lions kill their prey, but she's pretty sure it won't take long.

A blinding ray of light cuts shines into her eyes like a laser. She squints and leans forward, spotting a guard standing on the stairs a few rows in front of them. His shiny bronze helmet catches the sunlight and reflects it across the crowd, disorienting a few spectators as he moves his head.

Her face shifts with sudden inspiration. She leaps to her feet, startling Gaia. Aello, miraculously, still naps peacefully in her mistress's lap.

"What are you doing?" Gaia asks.

"Saving Liam," Aria says, already sliding out of the row toward the stairs.

The crowd grumbles and hisses as she squeezes past, but she doesn't stop. She reaches the stairs and stops two steps above the guard. She leans in, arms outstretched, inching her fingers closer to his head so she can reach the helmet.

The guard claps loudly, cheering the fight, and Aria uses the distraction to snatch the helmet off his head. She dives back into the crowd, keeping her head low until she gets back to her seat.

Gaia opens her mouth to speak, but Aria hushes her. She lifts the helmet and angles it so its smooth surface catches the sun.

When she angles the helmet just right, the reflection it creates is so powerful it almost looks like magic. Without losing focus, Aria directs the beam of light straight at the lion's face. She uses it like a spotlight, and the concentrated beam sends the animal into a frenzy. It lets out a roar and jerks its head back, trying to escape the assault.

Aria shifts the helmet a little and guides the light to the lion's paws. The animal stumbles, unsure of where to look, and begins to move frantically side-to-side, as if the floor were made of fire.

Aria bites her lip to keep from giggling, but other spectators don't bother to hide their amusement, and the crowd breaks out in laughter. If Liam's life wasn't in danger, it might've been one of the funniest things she's ever seen.

Liam's nose nearly scrapes the ground, and the dust from the sand floods his lungs. He pushes himself up onto his hands and knees, and what he sees makes his mouth fall open. The lion's jaws are no longer near. Instead, the animal sways from side to side, like it's performing the latest trendy dance.

Liam searches around for his arrow and spots it lying not too far away.

A boost of adrenaline gives him a focus so sharp it blocks out the noise of the screaming crowd. He jumps up, rising a few inches off the ground before landing solidly on his feet. He picks up his bow. He runs to retrieve his arrow and, in one swift motion, snatches it up and nocks it to the string.

A cloud slides over the sun, and the Colosseum darkens.

The lion stops moving.

It lets out a roar—not of pain, but of pure defiance.

It licks its muzzle once and charges at Liam.

FIFTY-EIGHT
THE GLADIATORS

With his gaze fixed on the lion, Liam lifts his bow and draws the string. The wild animal runs at him so fast its paws barely touch the ground.

The arrow flies across the arena and lands deep in the lion's side. The wound makes the animal howl in pain, but against all odds, it doesn't stop charging. On the contrary, it only fuels the creature's fury, making it unstoppable. Liam, now unarmed, braces himself for a brutal hand-to-paw fight.

But Titus emerges from the lion's shadow, running as fast as the wild animal. He gains momentum and plunges his sword into the lion's other flank. The animal lets out a cry, part anger, part surrender, and collapses to the ground just feet away from Liam.

The two boys stare at the wounded animal, frozen. The sound of the lion's pained breathing gives Liam goosebumps. He feels relief for his safety, but the creature's suffering crushes his heart.

The world rushes back in, and he hears the noise of the crowd again—cheers and stomping feet fill the Colosseum. The same crowd that booed them moments earlier is now celebrating them. The change is dizzying.

Liam stumbles to Titus on heavy legs. He takes Titus's hand, and they raise their arms into the air. The amphitheater explodes in applause. Liam and Titus finish their round of salutes, facing the aristocrats' box. Caius and Tiro applaud while exchanging a few words. *They must be discussing our freedom,* Liam thinks with relief.

"Silence!" Caius's voice cuts through the uproar. The crowd continues making noise until the trumpets blare, quieting them at last.

"People of Rome!" the senator bellows. "What a spectacle! I didn't expect those boys to survive, let alone triumph. Congratulations, Liam and Titus."

The spectators erupt in applause again, but the sound dies as soon as Caius raises both hands.

"However, the rule of the game is clear: To win your freedom, the lion must not draw another breath. And as you can all hear, it's still alive. The game is not over, and neither is the fight."

The crowd makes their displeasure with Caius's decision clear by booing. Liam's jaw tightens at the senator's words. How can Caius say this? Okay, they didn't kill the lion, but why take the life of an animal that never chose to be here?

Caius stands firm, unfazed by the unrest.

"I understand your irritation, citizens of Rome," he calls out over the rising complaints. "But I do not make the rules." The jeers grow louder. "The lion is wounded, so he won't be able to fight tomorrow. Therefore, the two boys will fight each other tomorrow until one dies. The survivor will be set free."

That announcement wins the crowd back. Their cheers return, loud and eager for more blood.

But for Liam and Titus, the words hit harder than any blow they've taken. One of them will have to die for the other to live.

The gate to the arena's backstage opens. Two guards emerge and seize the boys, who are no longer prisoners but are not free either. They are caught in a limbo neither of them asked for.

They walk off the field, unshackled but still caged. The shouts of the crowd fade behind them and their dream of freedom slips even farther away.

Liam's only thought is that he wants to live, but not at the cost of Titus's life.

FIFTY-NINE
THE TWIST

Aria and Gaia leave the Colosseum's stands filled with Romans calling for more blood. It's now time for Spartacus to fight against Achilles, and they have no wish to see that.

Aria bounds down the stairs leading to the exit two at a time. She nearly fainted from joy when Liam and Titus won, but a moment later, Caius's decision left her speechless. A rematch. Against each other.

How could he do this? How could he turn their victory into a death sentence?

"This way, Aria!" Gaia calls with Aello tucked safely in her arms.

Aria looks up to discover she's started down the wrong corridor. The Colosseum feels like a maze, especially since her mind is already lost.

"We need to find a way to get them out of the jail," Aria says as she catches up. "We can't let tomorrow's match happen."

"What will we do if we can't free them?" Gaia says.

Aria bites her lip. This is the first time in her life she can't accept a plan B. There's only one plan: Save Liam and Titus. "Nothing, because we *will* find a way."

"Maybe we can talk to Caius and convince him to change his mind. Why would he make them fight each other after they'd already won?"

"I'm trying to understand why," Aria says. "Did you see..." She stops herself, remembering who Gaia is. She had almost asked if Gaia noticed Tiro leaning toward Caius's ear, again and again, as if Caius were the puppet and Tiro the one holding the strings.

"Did I see what?" Gaia asks as they exit the Colosseum.

"Nothing, just there must be a reason behind it all, but—"

They both stop. Oliverus is waiting in front of them.

"Leave us alone," Gaia says as they pass him.

"Did Liam and Titus win?" he asks, catching up.

"Yes. Are you disappointed?" Gaia says sharply.

"I'm happy they're free," Oliverus says. "I would

never have forgiven myself if something awful happened to them."

Gaia stops and spins on Oliverus. "They aren't free! They have to fight again tomorrow! Each other!" she shouts. She's so close to his face, her breath hits his nose. Still, he doesn't step back. "So now only one of them will survive! They will have to kill one another!" Her anger spills out, unstoppable.

"Why? I... I'm so sorry... I will help you," Oliverus stammers.

Aria narrows her eyes at him. "What are you playing at now?"

"I know you have no reason to trust me," he says, looking at the ground, unable to meet her gaze. "But I really want to fix my mistakes. And there's something you have to know."

"Go on," Aria presses.

"You're seriously going to listen to him?" Gaia asks her.

"We'll hear him out, then decide what we think," Aria says, waving her hand in a circle at Oliverus to urge him to go on.

"Thank you," he says. "I've been awful to you, all of you. I feel terrible about it. But I can't let anything bad happen to you."

"What do you mean?" Aria asks.

Oliverus glances around, making sure no one can hear them. "Someone's trying to kill you both to stop you from helping Liam and Titus escape. They have to do the job before the dinner at your house, Gaia, tonight."

What he's saying hits Aria like a bomb. How could someone want them dead so badly? She looks around, a creepy feeling sneaking over her. She has the sensation Oliverus is telling the truth, but she wishes he weren't. Now, on top of saving Liam and Titus, they also have to make sure they aren't murdered.

"Are you trying to scare us so we won't ruin your father's plan?" Gaia asks, her tone making it clear she already knows the answer.

Oliverus flinches. "No! My father has nothing to do with Liam and Titus's fate. He's at home. He didn't vote for any of this!"

Gaia clenches her fists and holds her breath, as if that could keep the rage from breaking free. "Your father is the reason Liam and Titus are in this mess in the first place. He might have not asked for the rematch, but he condemned them to the Colosseum before any investigation could be done."

"My father didn't order this punishment. He was the

only senator who voted for a fair trial with Caesar, who still believes that Titus has nothing to do with his attack. I know because I heard my father discuss it with my mother."

Aria's face tightens. "That means Tiro voted to send Liam and Titus into the arena," she says.

Gaia lets out a choked cry. Aello slips from her arms, and Aria catches the tiny dog before she hits the ground. She lowers Aello gently, and the dog stretches her back legs.

"I guess so," Oliverus says. "But I know something else too."

"We're listening," Aria replies.

"The person who wants you dead also wants Caesar dead, tonight at the dinner."

"And why should we believe you?" Gaia asks.

"You don't have to," Oliverus says. "But not trusting me could cost you your lives, Liam's, Titus's, and Caesar's too. I can't save them on my own. That's a lot of lives to risk."

Aria crosses her arms over her chest. "Why did you change your mind and decide to help us?"

Oliverus bends forward a little, as though carrying an invisible weight. "I know I've been mean to you, all of you, and that I'm responsible for a lot of your trouble.

But I never did any of it out of hatred. I was jealous of you and of what you have. I didn't know how to be anyone other than the person I was. And when I finally realized that my behavior was the cause of my own pain, I knew I couldn't keep doing it. That's why I want to help you, as a first step to show that I'm sorry and that I want to change."

Aria pulls Gaia aside.

"I don't trust him," Gaia says. "This is a trap. He's just trying to get us arrested. He's playing us again!"

Aria glances back at Oliverus. He looks so different now. His arrogance is gone, and he now appears consumed by remorse.

"I can help free Liam and Titus," Oliverus adds. "My father donates a lot of money to the prison, so the guards know me. I'll tell them I want an autograph from Liam and Titus. They won't refuse me this favor."

Aria whispers to Gaia. "I get your point, but too many lives are at risk."

"But Aria…"

"Think about it. We don't have a better plan. He can get us into the prison. Once inside, we can find a way to sneak Liam and Titus out. His plan's actually better than mine."

"And if it's a setup?"

Aria shrugs. "Then we're done. We die, Caesar dies tonight, the wrong man takes power, and Rome perishes. And Liam or Titus joins us in the realm of death."

Gaia stares at her, eyes wide and mouth open so far that a bee could fly right in.

"Glad we agree," Aria says, already turning back to Oliverus. "I hope you're worthy of our trust," she says to him.

"I am. The prison entrance is this way. We shouldn't waste time. And don't forget to keep an eye on your surroundings."

Aria feels an odd wave of relief to be in this era. At least she doesn't have to worry about guns. If someone wants to kill her, they'll have to get close. It's the kind of thought she never imagined would ever cross her mind.

"Follow my lead and don't forget to play the part," Oliverus tells Aria and Gaia as they head toward the prison's gate.

"What do we do once we are with Titus and Liam? At least one guard will probably stay with us," Gaia says.

"I have an idea," Aria replies with a wink.

SIXTY

THREE DEATHS

Outside the Colosseum, Mogurix takes cover behind the trunk of a tree. Thanks to his small portions of food that resulted in his skinny frame, he doesn't need much to stay hidden.

He grips the handle of his dagger. The two girls are only a few feet away—close enough for him to catch the faint echo of their conversation, but too far for a discreet attack.

There's a boy with them. To keep his identity hidden, the boy must die too. A stab of guilt hits Mogurix, but he forces it down. He cannot be a coward now. His master was clear about his orders, and Mogurix knows it's the only option he has if he wants to remain in his master's service.

Mogurix pulls his hood back on. He will charge, head low and steady in his pace, strike Gaia first, then Aria, then the boy. Three quick moves for three quick deaths.

With his plan set, he steps out from his hiding place.

SIXTY-ONE

THE SUSPECTS

Liam and Titus are back in their cell, one of them a day away from death, the other from becoming a killer. Everything feels dark and rough, stripped of joy and life.

"I can't believe we're back in this place!" Titus bursts out.

"At least we're not yet dead," Liam says, more to cheer himself than Titus.

"I can't believe Caius did this to us! Put us against each other, for what? We should have been freed. We deserved it!"

"Maybe he did it to help us."

Titus scowls. "Are you mad? I think you hit more than your butt when that lion threw you off its back."

"Okay, I know my theory sounds crazy. But if

Septimus wants to frame us for Caesar's murder, he can't do it while we're in jail. He would need us to be free before he kills Caesar, so we can be accused again. That's why being locked up right now might be for our own good."

Titus gives him a look, as if wondering whether he's lost his mind. "And why would he make us fight each other in a rematch until one of us dies? That's pure evil."

"Probably because he doesn't want to draw attention by going in our favor. He might plan to release us before the match once it is safe for us."

"Your optimism will kill you one day, you know that."

The jail door opens. Spartacus appears with a guard, who unlocks their cell.

"I'm proud of you both," the gladiator says, stepping inside. His arms are marked with several fresh cuts. "I never thought you'd fight so bravely. You clearly have gladiator blood in you."

"Hah, I'm not so sure," Liam replies. "If it wasn't for that magical beam of light, the lion would've eaten me alive."

"I told you the gods would help you," Spartacus says. "And don't ever downplay what you've done. You two make a great team."

If only they could be a team in something that didn't involve fighting.

Spartacus sits on his bench with a heavy sigh. "I know you two must be frightened about tomorrow."

"Frightened? That's a small word. I don't want to kill anyone just to survive," Liam says.

"You don't always have to. The senator in charge decides. Today, Achilles and I didn't fight to the death. Imagine if every match ended with a gladiator dying. There wouldn't be any of us left."

"So you think Caius's decision could be reversed tomorrow if another senator is in charge?" Titus asks.

"If you give them enough of a show, yes."

"Then we will!" Liam says, looking at Titus with hope.

Once again, the door to their section swings open. Liam covers his ears; that grating sound is unbearable. Then a voice he despises chills him to the bone.

SIXTY-TWO
THE SHOUTS

ogurix runs away from the Colosseum, away from the cheering crowds, his legs moving on their own.

He was only a few feet from the trio, ready to strike, when the crowd erupted into a screaming frenzy. The sound hit him like a blow, dizzying and unbearable.

The roar of the spectators pounds in his head, too close to the cries of the Romans who stormed his village. His chest burns; it feels as if his lungs are slamming against each other, no air moving in or out. The noise grows louder and louder until he thinks he might go deaf.

The sun is sinking behind the buildings. Soon, night will fall. Mogurix has lost all sense of time. He must have run for hours.

He slows and tries to catch his breath. The shouts have faded, and little by little, his mind clears. Then his master's voice rushes back: *Now kill the two girls before the dinner tonight.* Even this, Mogurix failed to do. And worse still, the words that haunted him—*You're just a useless waste of coin*—sting sharper than ever.

He grabs his head and screams silently. What should he do now?

The dinner. Yes. That's where he should go. To stand beside his master as he asked. To prove his worth.

With trembling resolve, Mogurix forces his legs to carry him toward the Carina villa.

SIXTY-THREE

THE END OF THE GAME

"What a show!" Tiro exclaims as he walks beside Caius out of the main entrance of the Colosseum. "Spartacus and Achilles played wonderfully well. I haven't seen anything so exciting in ages. Too bad Marcia didn't join us as planned; she would've loved it. But she takes her hostess duties seriously, and organizing the dinner is all she can think about right now."

The sun begins to set behind the Colosseum, dragging its light away from the city.

"Marcia is the best hostess in Rome; you should be proud," Caius says. "We should hurry to your house if we don't want to be late and risk her scolding."

"You know her well." Tiro winks.

A two-wheeled chariot, complete with a curved

wooden front reinforced with bronze panels, approaches the front of the building. Two horses trot steadily, their harnesses jingling.

"Here comes my chariot," Caius says. The horses stop in front of them. "Epo," he calls to the driver, "light the torch and guide our way."

Epo nods, grabs an unlit torch from the chariot, and steps down. He bows to Caius, who climbs aboard and takes the reins, with Tiro joining him at his side. A few paces away, a torch burns by the drop-off line. Epo uses it to light his own before returning to the chariot.

Caius gives the reins a shake, and the horses surge forward with Epo running by their side to light the way.

"I have to say," Tiro continues, "I was surprised you decided to keep the two criminals for tomorrow's event. But I'm grateful. Letting them run free in Rome? Unthinkable."

One of the wheels slams into a rock, jolting the chariot so hard it nearly tips. "Do your job!" Caius snaps at Epo. With the sun almost gone and no moon to be seen, the road lies in darkness, and the boy hasn't kept far enough ahead to light the way.

"Finding good slaves gets harder and harder these days," Caius mutters, and Tiro nods his approval. Fortunately, they reach the Carina estate in one piece.

Tiro climbs down first, with Caius just behind him. Inside the house, it looks like a volcano is erupting. Servants rush back and forth carrying plates, jars, and barrels. A man lights a line of oil lamps just as Marcia bursts into the vestibule, her hair in disarray as if she has just woken up.

"Tiro!" Marcia exclaims. "I'm so sorry for the mess. It seems that we all fell asleep. I woke only a few minutes ago … and now we have to prepare everything for tonight. Oh, Caius, you're already here."

Caius's lips curve upward. "Yes, but don't worry about me. I know your skill as a hostess and won't judge you for this."

Marcia lets out a sigh of relief. "Thank you. I don't know why I slept so long, but how could everyone else here do the same? That's a far more worrying question!"

"Where is Gaia?" asks Tiro.

Marcia jumps. "Oh! I've been so busy giving orders, I forgot to check on her. I'll go now." She glances around, as if overwhelmed by the endless tasks yet to be done.

"It's all right, Marcia," Tiro says. "Keep preparing, and I will go see her."

Her shoulders loosen as she smiles and walks into the living room, shouting to Faustina to adjust one of the flower bouquets.

SIXTY-FOUR
THE GETAWAY CART

In his cell, Liam rolls his eyes and sneers. Oliverus's voice gets under his skin, and he hates himself for letting it.

"One autograph and that's it," a guard says in a tone that's falsely sweet.

"My father wouldn't like you speaking to me with such harshness," Oliverus snaps back.

A door slams, its echo shaking the hallway. Then comes an even worse sound—a bonk, followed by an "ow." Liam stiffens.

"Well done," Oliverus's voice drifts in.

"I told you my plan was genius." Aria's voice sounds as refreshing as a mountain stream.

Liam rushes to the bars of the cell. Titus joins him with the same frantic and hopeful energy.

"Aria, is that you?" Liam dares to ask.

"Of course it's me. Who else would come save your butt?"

A few seconds later, he sees her come out of the corridor.

Joy surges through him. He has never been so happy to see her. Even the times she surprised him with his favorite dessert don't compare to this moment.

"Did you miss me?" Aria beams.

"Heck yeah!" Liam lets out, then turns serious. "Did you knock out the guard?"

"We sure did," Gaia says, stepping out from Aria's shadow with Aello at her side.

"Gaia!" Titus exclaims, and everyone shushes him. "Sorry," he mutters.

Gaia lifts her hand and rattles a set of keys. "And we stole this." She hurries to the cell door and unlocks it. It's barely ajar when Titus flings it wide open and throws himself into her arms.

Liam follows right after and squeezes Aria until she can barely breathe.

Oliverus coughs. "Hate to interrupt the reunion, but we should hurry before another guard checks on us."

Liam breaks his hug with Aria and says, "Is he serious? What is he even doing here?"

"Be nice, Liam," Aria says, surprising him with her change of heart. "He's the reason we made it into the prison."

Titus turns to Spartacus. "Are you coming with us?"

The gladiator rises to meet them. "No, I belong here. This will be my life until I win my freedom."

"What?" Liam blurts.

Spartacus pulls him into a hug and claps him warmly on the back. "Good luck." Then he steps back into the cell, closing the door behind him and sealing himself inside.

"How do we get out of here?" Titus asks. "We can't just walk out like this; we'll be recognized."

"We thought about that," Gaia replies. "One of you will wear the uniform of the guard we knocked out. There's another guard in the next section. We call him over, trap him, and bam! Then the other one of you gets his outfit. After that, we use the keys to move through each section of the jail until we're out."

"I like this new Gaia," Titus says with a wink.

Liam frowns at Aria, stunned. "Are you crazy?"

Aria sighs. "Come on, Liam, don't be such a wimp. It's a brilliant plan."

"Do you even know what *brilliant* means, Aria?"

"I'll take this man's uniform," Titus says as he looks at

the unconscious guard. "I've worn this filthy tunic for far too long." With Oliverus's help, he's soon transformed into a Roman Vigiles.

Titus moves to stand behind the door leading to the next section. "Everyone ready?" he whispers. They all nod, and he knocks on the door.

The lock clicks, and the door cracks open.

"Can … can you come in here?" Titus says, lowering his voice to sound like the fallen guard.

"What now?" the guard says from the other side, annoyed.

Titus eases the door wider and leans against the wall. The guard steps in, and Titus slams the door shut. Liam and Oliverus leap on him from both sides, while Aria scrambles onto his back and presses her fingers to his temples.

"What are you doing?" Liam says as he struggles to hold the guard, who howls in pain.

"It's a pressure point. It'll knock him out," Aria says, forcing her fingers to stay in place.

At last, the guard's body goes slack. He collapses to the floor, taking Aria down with him.

She pushes herself back up, chest heaving. "Easy peasy."

Liam just stares at her, speechless. "I learned this in karate class," Aria says quickly, feeling the need to explain.

"Come on, Liam. Get changed and let's get out of here," Titus says.

Liam feels confident wearing the Roman armor. It's rigid but protective, a welcome change from his flimsy tunic. The only thing he could do without is the ridiculous red-feather crest bobbing on top of the helmet.

Liam and Titus take the front of the procession and try to avoid eye contact with prisoners as they pass through each section. They attempt to mimic the stiff, self-important strut they've seen all the guards do. They are so close to freedom that now is not the time to slip up.

At the gate, Oliverus greets the stationed guards with a slight bow. "These two will escort me home," Oliverus says, tilting his head in Liam and Titus's direction. "And perhaps you could spare us two of your chariots. It's dark, and my father wouldn't be pleased if I took too long getting back."

"But they belong to the city of Rome," the guard objects.

Oliverus lifts his chin and looks straight at the guard.

"Do you dare say they aren't good enough for the son of a dictator?"

They rush to obey.

SIXTY-FIVE
THE TOAST

Marcia hears the bell at the villa's front gate ring and rushes to greet her new guest.

"Septimus, I'm glad to see you," she says, flashing a smile that doesn't quite reach her eyes. "I must apologize for the mess. It seems the entire household took long naps today. We're terribly behind."

"I'm sure it is not as bad as you claim," Septimus replies. "I've brought a small gift."

Marcia leans sideways to watch a man roll a barrel into the house. It looks heavier than a boulder. "Oh, thank you. That's so thoughtful. Tiro and Caius are waiting for you in the living room."

Septimus thanks her and heads to the room. Tiro comes to greet him on the landing. "Septimus! I hope you're feeling better."

"Much better." Septimus shakes Tiro's hand before turning to Caius. "Thank you for filling in at the games. My wife told me about the two boys and your decision to keep them for tomorrow."

Caius bows. "I did my best to handle it as you would have."

"I should remind you that I voted for a trial. Those boys don't deserve to die in the arena when their culpability hasn't been proven," Septimus says dryly.

Tiro waves a hand to dismiss such a silly idea. "Why waste time and money on criminals?"

"If they're the wrong criminals—"

"Caesar, my friend, you're here!" Tiro interrupts them and rushes to meet the latest guest.

"Thank you for your warm welcome," Caesar says, shaking Tiro's hand. "I've spent the last few days buried in work, so I welcome the diversion." He joins Caius and Septimus, shaking their hands in turn. "Are we expecting any additional guests?"

"More will join later. I wanted to see you three first," Tiro replies, picking up a bell from a nearby side table. "But before we dig into business, let's toast to a bright future for Rome." He rings it, and Faustina arrives at once.

"Please serve us some wine," Tiro says.

"If I may," Septimus says, raising a finger. "I brought my latest vintage as a thank-you for your hospitality." He turns to the living room entrance and calls, "Simplicius, bring the barrel."

A man appears in the doorway with a barrel almost too wide to pass through. He rolls it forward and stops a few feet from the group. Faustina grabs a jar and kneels by the barrel, reaching for the tap to pour wine, but Tiro stops her.

"That's kind of you, Septimus, but I insist on offering my vintage for the first round," says Tiro.

"Come now," Caius says to Tiro. "Let's drink Septimus's wine."

"Yes," Caesar adds, "I have never tried Septimus's vintage. And I'm in the mood for something new."

Septimus locks his gaze with Tiro's unblinking eyes. Slowly, a smile spreads across Septimus's face. It's not a warm one, but rather one of quiet satisfaction. It is the kind of smile that appears when everything begins to unfold exactly as planned.

SIXTY-SIX

THE PUZZLE PIECES

Titus climbs into one of the two chariots generously provided by the Roman Vigiles.

Oliverus says to Liam, "You need to drive the other, or the guards will be suspicious."

"Or I can do it," Aria shoots back, but Liam raises his hand in front of her. "Oliverus is right. I'd better do it." He steps into the second chariot, leaving Aria gaping behind him.

"We should take different routes," Titus says. "If there's still an assassin after us, it'll be harder for him to find us."

Oliverus nods. "Good idea. I'll go with Aria and Liam to show them the way to Gaia's house."

"Gaia, come with me," Titus says, and Gaia climbs aboard, taking Aello with her.

"See you there," he calls, snapping the reins. His horses leap forward.

Aria scrambles into the chariot next to Liam and makes room for Oliverus. He can barely get his footing before Liam orders the horses forward.

"Aria, I need to tell you something," Liam says.

"What is it? You sound serious."

"I think you were right."

Aria's eyes bulge. She taps her ear.

"What are you doing?" Liam asks.

"Just checking if my ears are working."

Liam rolls his eyes. "They are."

"And what exactly am I right about?"

Liam starts to answer, but the words die on his lips when he remembers Oliverus is standing beside her. How could he accuse Oliverus's father right in front of the man's son? Liam leans closer to Aria. "I think Septimus is the culprit."

"What?" Aria says. "I didn't hear you. Can you speak louder?"

Liam repeats the words in her ear.

"Liam, stop!" Aria yells.

Liam jerks back and yanks the reins. The chariot screeches to a halt. His heart races so fast he thinks it might burst. Two men shout at him angrily as they finish crossing the street. It was a close call.

"Be careful! You're going to kill someone," Oliverus says.

"At least I wouldn't do it on purpose, unlike your father," Liam fires back, and the regret hits him at once. He isn't a bully. Why does Oliverus bring that out in him?

"My father is innocent!" says Oliverus.

"I hate to break it to you, Liam," Aria says, "but I think you were right when you challenged our theory. Septimus isn't guilty, at least I don't think so."

"He's not," agrees Oliverus. "He didn't vote for Titus and you to end up in the arena."

"But Tiro did," Aria says.

Liam gulps. "What? How? Gaia's father?"

"Yes," she continues. "First clue: Gaia told him about the murder plot, and he did nothing except send guards after her."

"Are you sure?" Oliverus says to Aria. "Do you really think he would try to kill his own daughter?"

"Unfortunately, it looks like he did. He was the only one Gaia talked to," Aria says. "Second, he lied about sharing the same political beliefs as Caesar, and I know he argued with him about the new policy he wanted to pass. Third, he was whispering to Caius during the games. He must be the one who convinced him to condemn you to a rematch. That's why I believe Tiro is guilty. Everything points to him."

"And why would he do it?" Liam asks.

"To get out of the blackmail scam he came up with! Remember, Gaia told us her family was never blackmailed. That's because Tiro was behind the scam. And he knew about the conversation Titus overheard at the tavern."

"He was blackmailed," Liam counters. "Titus told me. Apparently, the blackmailer knew about the most embarrassing thing that has ever happened to Gaia's family. It must be why she didn't tell us. She is ashamed."

"Really? What was his secret?" Aria asks.

"Titus wouldn't say."

"Gambling," Oliverus cuts in.

"How do you know?" Liam asks.

"Everyone in Rome learned about the senators' secrets during the blackmailing scandal. Tiro gambled at card games and nearly lost the family fortune."

Aria slaps her forehead. "That must be why he fought with Caesar. Tiro argued with Caesar about his plan to raise taxes on the senators. Because of Tiro's gambling problem, he probably didn't want to pay more because he *couldn't*. It's hard to stop an addiction, so he likely kept gambling and didn't have enough money to give to the state."

"That's bad," Liam says.

"But still better than being a murderer," Aria replies.

"Okay, maybe we need to look at this from another angle," Liam says. "If Septimus isn't guilty—"

"And he isn't," Oliverus interrupts.

"Fine, yes," Liam goes on. "That means the real culprit is framing Septimus. So he isn't just getting rid of Caesar, he's getting rid of Septimus too." The weight of his words sinks in, and Liam shivers. You'd have to be crazy to come up with a plan like that. "So who benefits? That's the answer we need."

Aria freezes, caught in a moment where everything suddenly fits together. "It's Caius!"

"Are you sure? Why?" Liam presses.

"He has a strong motive. He wants to become a dictator. But with Septimus already elected and Caesar on the verge of becoming one too, he knows the Senate won't approve a third. So he needs both of them out of the way. And he's probably the one who framed Titus's father."

"But he was scammed too! Titus told me his wife left him because of it," Liam protests.

"He didn't seem very sad about it," Oliverus cuts in. "I remember him looking almost relieved. They never got along."

Aria presses her lips together, furious with herself. "Now I remember. How did I not realize it sooner!"

"What?" Oliverus asks.

"Gaia told me Caius was with her father when she warned him about the murder plot Titus overheard. She said he almost believed her."

Liam stares ahead, the truth sinking in. "Great. I'm just as clueless."

"No, you're not," Aria says quickly. "We just didn't have all the pieces before."

"I am. I thought Caius was protecting Titus and me by keeping us in jail, so the real culprit couldn't act without clearing us and Caesar would stay safe. But in truth, he wants Titus and me dead, so Titus can't identify Caius's henchman. Titus saw too much."

"Yes," Aria continues. "And he will murder Caesar at the dinner tonight and accuse Septimus."

"That's evil," Oliverus says.

"Yes, but we won't let him succeed." Liam tightens his grip on the reins and snaps them. The horses surge forward, racing to close the gap between them and the Carina villa.

SIXTY-SEVEN
THE MEMORY

Outside the Carina villa, Mogurix crouches beneath the open window that looks into the living room. He studies the inside of the room, and his face splits into a smile when he sees his master. *There he is.*

Now he just has to wait for orders. Settling down, he listens to the senators' conversation. They're arguing about wine. What an odd thing to fight over. Then again, Mogurix finds every topic absurd to fight about. He doesn't like fighting at all.

The sound of his master's voice drifts out the window and fills him with a sense of safety. To Mogurix, it's like a melody.

"Tiro, Septimus's slave worked hard to bring the barrel here. The least we can do is try it."

"Exactly," says Septimus.

"By the way, Caius," Caesar says, "would you be willing to sell me the slave you mentioned? Our household has gotten more complicated, and we might need an extra hand."

"Mogurix?" Caius says.

At the sound of his name, Mogurix's chest tightens, terror pushing aside his joy.

"Yes, I'll consider selling him," Caius continues. "But let me tell you, he's a useless man. I did my best to make him somewhat valuable, but nothing worked. You can have him for fifty."

"Fifty?' Mogurix whispers to himself.

A scream starts to rise from his stomach. It builds and builds, then slips out of his mouth without a sound. He pushes himself up, but the world is hazy. Tears blur his eyes. His mouth opens, yet no voice comes. Just like him, silent and unseen.

He stumbles, bracing himself against the house wall. His strength is gone. He breathes, but feels dead, existing in a place worse than this earth. His stomach twists with cries he cannot release.

And then he sees her. Her face. Her smile. The shouts of Roman soldiers roar in his mind, but over them lingers his mother's melodious voice.

"Mogurix, I love you more than you will ever know. Always and forever. You must be strong for your mother. You must fight, fight for the life you deserve. I cannot escape. I must protect the village. But you must leave and never come back!"

He remembers her words now, truly remembers them, and along with them comes the warmth of her love. It fills him for a moment, the way it once did when he was a child. She didn't want him to leave because she did not love him. She told him to leave so that he could live free from the Romans' control. And in that truth, he feels the sharp contrast of what he has known since: a life without love, a life in chains.

A deep sound rises within him. His cry breaks through the silence, rough and powerful, scattering the birds into the sky.

For the first time in years, he feels the weight lift. He feels free. Free to go, free to walk away from the place that taught him blind obedience instead of affection. He can finally see the world as it really is.

His fingers brush the tag fastened to the iron collar around his neck, the one engraved: *Hold me, lest I flee, and return me to my master Caius.*

He gives a last glance at the living room. Then he turns and walks away.

This time, he leaves, and he will never come back.

✳ 307 ✳

SIXTY-EIGHT
THE CULPRIT

Caius takes the jar from Faustina's hand and picks up a glass from the table beside them. A scream from outside sends goosebumps down every guest's arms. All eyes turn to the row of windows facing the garden, but the darkness reveals nothing.

"It must be an animal in the stables," Tiro says.

Caius's lips curl into a smile as his fingers tighten around the wine jar. "Thank you, Faustina. I'll take it from here."

"Fifty is a deal," Caesar says as he accepts the glass of wine Caius offers him.

Caius pours two more glasses and hands them to Septimus and Tiro before serving himself. "A toast to friendship." He raises his glass.

"To the senators of Rome," Caesar says, lifting his own.

Septimus and Tiro echo the toast.

Just as the glasses touch their lips, a voice shouts at them from the living room entrance.

"Caesar, be careful!"

The senators gasp at the sight of Aria, Oliverus, and a Roman guard bursting in.

"Oliverus, what is the meaning of this interruption?" Septimus bellows, his voice shaking the walls.

Liam removes his helmet, and the room erupts in shock. "Caesar, someone is trying to kill you!" he says.

Caesar looks around. "Someone help this boy. He's clearly lost his mind."

Tiro blinks. "But ... how did you escape from jail?" When Titus and Gaia run into the living room, Tiro freezes, eyes wide, as if he's seen a ghost.

"Finally, you're here," Aria says to the newcomers.

"Wait, we took the shortest route. How did you get here before us?" Titus asks.

"I know a shortcut," Oliverus replies.

"Gaia, I thought you were in your room!" Tiro says in disbelief.

"What is the meaning of this?" Caesar asks.

"Caesar, Caius wants to kill you!" Aria shouts with all her strength.

Every eye turns to Caius, whose smile has vanished. His face darkens like a storm cloud.

Caius lets out a cold laugh that makes Aria's skin prickle. "Me? Why would I try to kill my friend? You think you're a clever little girl, but you're not. It was Septimus, with the help of these two rascals." He glares at Liam and Titus.

He lifts his glass and points it straight at Septimus. "And I believe he was going to try again tonight."

Suspicion spreads like smoke, thick and choking, as each man looks to the next, unsure where the truth lies.

SIXTY-NINE
THE EVIDENCE

"You're all making a mistake," Caius says as he sets his glass on the table and strides up to Septimus with defiance. He stands as tall as he can, yet still barely reaches the man's chest. "I wouldn't be surprised if Septimus slipped something into the wine just to get rid of his biggest rivals all at once."

Septimus bites his lower lip. "It's *you*," he says to Caius. "How did I not see it before?"

Caesar looks down at his glass. His hand begins to tremble. "Septimus, is it true?"

"No, I swear." Septimus lifts his own glass and drinks it down in one gulp. "If my wine was poisoned, do you think I would drink it?"

"Then why did you bring it?" Tiro asks.

"Because I thought you were going to poison Caesar with your wine. I was trying to protect him."

"You think I'm behind the murder plot?" Tiro asks, pain in his voice.

"I guess I was wrong," Septimus replies. "Caius was second on my suspect list."

"I did nothing!" Caius insists. "Septimus, if you are so innocent, drink Caesar's wine."

"Why would I do that? You're the one who poured it. You could've put something in it."

Caius's jaw drops, but he quickly regains his composure. "I did no such thing."

"Then you won't mind if we search your pockets," Aria says.

"No one touches me. I'm a senator."

"I'm sorry about all this, Caius," Caesar says, stepping forward and clapping him on the back. "I know you're innocent."

"Now listen to me!" Liam shouts, putting every bit of force he has left into his voice.

Everyone stares at him, unsure if they should be scared or just surprised.

Liam continues now he's got the attention of the room. "I'm sick and tired of all this drama! Titus and I risked our lives in the arena to save you, Caesar, so the least you could do is hear us out. Believe me, I'd rather be having fun in Sommet—I mean, Alexandria—than be stuck in your ridiculous conspiracy story. The whole thing feels like a preschool game! So stop being stubborn and listen!"

No one speaks.

"All right," Liam says, breathing hard. "Now that I have your attention, I'll let Aria explain."

"Uh… Y-yes, of course," she stammers, still shocked by Liam's outburst. "As we were saying, Caius wants to kill you, Caesar. And we suspect he might be behind the scam that took down Titus's father."

"Scoundrel!" Titus shouts, lunging at Caius. Oliverus and Liam stop him just in time.

"You destroyed my family! I'll kill you!" Titus thrashes, but Oliverus holds him by the waist.

"I'll have you arrested for defamation!" Caius barks, jabbing a finger at Titus before turning to Aria.

Liam steps beside her. "Then drink Caesar's glass of wine if you're innocent."

"I know Septimus poisoned it, so I won't drink it. You won't get rid of me so you can get them to believe your ridiculous murder plot."

Septimus turns out his pockets. "I have nothing in

my pockets, and if we test the barrel, I can assure you that you will find no poison."

"Caius, show us what's in your pockets," Tiro says with authority.

"I have nothing to hide," Caius replies. "But I won't let anyone—"

"Caius, show us your pockets," Liam says.

Caius takes a step back.

"Show us," Tiro repeats.

"You're all mistaken!" Caius says, backing up again.

Marcia strides in with a smile far too bright. "I have some good news!" she announces, then stops short. Her expression darkens. "Did I miss something?"

No one responds. Everyone is too busy glaring at Caius.

SEVENTY

THE MOTIVE

Liam leans forward, bracing himself on one leg. He can tell Aria, still standing beside him, is tensing up too. The living room in the Carina villa feels frozen, like a scene trapped inside a painting.

In one sudden motion, Caius takes out a dagger from his belt.

"But … Caius…" Caesar stammers.

"Shut up!" Caius shouts. His voice is so cold and twisted it barely sounds like him.

"That's the voice I heard in front of the Colosseum!" Oliverus says.

"Nobody moves, or I'll strike!" Caius growls, brandishing the blade.

Marcia screams, and Tiro pulls her behind him to shield her.

Caius whirls like a madman, waving the dagger at each guest one by one, as if he's trying to control the entire room. There are too many people around him to escape, but the knife keeps everyone at bay.

Oliverus releases Titus, who asks, "Why did you frame my father?" His voice carries the pain and sadness he's felt ever since his father died.

Caius smirks. "Your father was an easy target. And I must say, his righteousness made the outcome all the sweeter. He always thought he was better than everyone. Always clinging to the rules."

"You destroyed my family for money," Titus spits.

"Not just for money," Caius sneers. "For the pleasure of watching senators squirm under my blackmail."

"You're evil," Tiro says.

Caius shrugs. "Like that's a bad thing?"

Liam's eyes drift to the barrel of wine. "Psst," he whispers to Aria. She turns, and he tilts his head at the barrel.

She nods in understanding, and before anyone can stop them, the two leap forward and shove the barrel as hard as they can toward the center of the room.

It rolls fast—too fast for Caius to get out of the way.

With a loud crash, it slams into his legs and knocks him off his feet. He lands flat on his back with a thud.

Septimus rushes in and pins Caius's arms. Tiro joins, grabbing the other side. Together, they hold the traitor down.

Tiro searches Caius's pockets, and he pulls out a small vial from one of them.

"I'm sure this is the proof we need," he says, handing the vial to Septimus. Septimus opens it, sniffs, and makes a face before slipping it into his pocket. Then he takes Caesar's glass, smells it, and jerks back.

"The vial holds aconite, and I can smell it in the glass too."

Caesar looks like he's been punched in the gut. "Why, Caius? I thought you were my friend."

"Give me a break," Caius sneers. "I deserve to rule. I should be the only dictator in Rome, not Septimus or you. Your ideas are stupid and will bring the Empire down. With me in charge, the world would belong to Rome. I'd conquer every land."

"I'm not so sure," Aria says.

"You think you are cleverer than everyone," Caius says to Aria. "But you are just a stupid little girl."

"Sorry, but remind me again, who's the one that got caught?" Liam fires back. "Oh, right. You. So maybe think twice before calling someone stupid."

"Guards!" Tiro calls out.

The Carinas' bodyguards storm in, grab Caius by the arm, and drag him from the room as if he weighs nothing.

"Ouch!" Caius protests, but no one bothers to check on him.

"Can you take care of him?" Tiro asks Septimus.

"I will," Septimus says. "We'll take him to prison until we've gathered all the evidence we need to guarantee his conviction."

"I can give you the name of his forger," Liam says to Septimus with pride.

"And what about his servant who attacked Caesar?" Aria asks. "We don't know where he is."

"He's a slave," Liam tells her. "Titus saw his collar or something, so maybe he's had punishment enough. It's not like he had a choice."

Aria smiles faintly. History feels very different here than it ever did in books.

SEVENTY-ONE
FATE

Everyone stands in the Carinas' living room, listening to Caius's screams fade into the distance, like a bad dream slipping away.

"I'll keep you both updated," Septimus says to Tiro and Caesar, who hasn't yet found his voice. Septimus turns to Aria, Liam, Titus, and Gaia. "And thank you, all of you."

"You're welcome," Aria replies. "But really, Oliverus was a huge help."

Septimus looks at his son and acknowledges the remark with a slight tilt of his head.

"When I invited you all for a drink before dinner, I wanted to discuss the possibility that someone wanted to murder Caesar," Tiro says, "but I never thought Caius was behind it."

"And he tried to kill me too," Gaia adds, drawing a horrified look from both her parents. She says to her father, "Yes, he sent guards after me because I told you about the plot."

"You were chased by guards?" Marcia says. Her face shows the kind of terror only a loving mother could display.

"Yes, but I lost them," Gaia explains, brushing off her mother's concern with a wave that only makes Marcia's jaw drop more.

"Anyway, I owe you all a great debt," Caesar says. "I never imagined someone would try to take my life. And that it would be a man I considered a close friend, no less." He walks to Titus. When he reaches him, he hesitates for a heartbeat before pulling him into a tight embrace. "I'm sorry, Titus. I missed you so much. I should have helped you and your mother after your father's death. I failed him."

Titus looks like a sausage squashed between two slices of bread until Caesar finally lets go. The boy nods in response, but no words come out.

Tiro seizes the silence. "I owe you both my sincerest apologies," he says to Liam and Titus. "To think you nearly died trying to save Rome."

"That's okay," Titus says. "We all make mistakes. What matters is that the truth came out."

"Titus," Tiro says, gripping his shoulder. "Now that the truth is out, we'll restore your family's honor and heritage. You can't stay living in the slums. Your place is among us."

"Many people live poorly. Why should I deserve better, just because of my family name?"

"He's right," Caesar says. "It's a problem we must face in Rome. Every citizen should have enough to eat and a decent place to sleep. We, the aristocrats, can't keep all the riches for ourselves. Once I become dictator, I'll work on that."

"Thank you," Titus says.

"Too much emotion. I'm going to cry," Liam whispers to Aria.

"It's time for us to go," Septimus says. "Come now, Oliverus."

"Yes, father."

"Wait," Marcia says. "Don't you want to stay for the party? The other guests should be here any minute."

Septimus looks puzzled, as do the others. "You still plan to have a party after all this?"

Marcia straightens and lifts her chin. "Of course. You've done your job, and now it's time to do mine.

With the servants, we have been working for days to prepare tonight's event. Plus, I won't turn people away after I've invited them."

"Well, when you put it like that… I guess we'd better put on bright faces and get ready to entertain," Tiro says.

"Managing a household is way harder than I thought," Aria says to Liam.

"And all these events to plan! I still have nightmares about my last birthday party. So many things to do, worse than a pile of homework!" Liam's weary tone makes Aria chuckle.

Gaia claps her hands. "Let's go play some games in my room."

"No gladiator games, I beg you," Liam says, earning laughter from the others.

On her way out of the living room, Gaia glances back. "Are you coming, Oliverus?" she asks the boy as he stands stiffly beside his father.

He touches his chest. "Me? You want me to hang out with you?"

"Yes," Gaia says.

For a moment, he just stares at her, then breaks into a grin and hurries to join them.

Liam falls in step with Aria. "Hopefully, our Oliver becomes a good guy too."

"Even if he doesn't, understanding why Oliverus was the way he was helped me understand Oliver too."

"We should be careful about this new traveling adventure thing. It's making you wiser than you should be for your own good."

Aria laughs and nudges him lightly.

A few minutes later, in Gaia's room, the group gathers around a wooden tray covered with polished stones.

"Come on, let's immortalize this moment," Liam says, pulling out his phone.

Oliverus squints at the phone. "I'm sorry, but what is that object?"

"Uh… Something from Alexandria. Doesn't matter. Just sit back and smile."

The group huddles together, everyone beaming happily.

"One, two, three!" Liam takes a photo.

As the shutter clicks, a servant enters the room.

"Pardon the interruption," he says shyly, looking at Aria. "But would it be possible to have another cup of your elixir of youth?"

Aria and Gaia burst out laughing as the boys exchange confused looks.

"Of course," Aria says. "We'll make it for you."

The man bows. "Thank you. I will wait for you in the garden."

Liam winces. "Elixir of youth? What is he talking about?"

"Nothing," Aria says, her tone too innocent to be true. "He just wants hot chocolate. I made them try your mom's recipe, and apparently, it had quite an effect."

"You didn't! Tell me you didn't give the recipe to anyone."

"Only to Faustina."

"We have to get it back! No one should make that recipe before my mom."

"Are you serious? It's like 60 BC. It's not going to end up in a cookbook."

"We can't take that risk. It brings her too much joy to know she's the only one to have the recipe."

He pulls Aria out of the room, then stops short as the warmth of the Carina villa vanishes.

They are standing in the empty hallway of Sommetville Junior High.

Aria and Liam look at each other. Their Roman outfits are gone, replaced by their usual gym clothes.

"We're back home," Liam says.

"It looks like it," Aria replies in awe.

"I wonder what happened to Gaia, Titus, and Oliverus."

"And Caesar! There's only one way to find out."

They push through the swinging doors and race out into the daylight until they reach the basketball courts. Oliver is there, holding Aria's notebook.

"Aria … I'm sorry about earlier," Oliver says, handing over her belongings. "Here you go."

"Thank you, Oliver. It's all forgotten," she says.

"That's it? You're not going to curse me out for what I did?"

"No. I won't, because I'm sure you'll try to do the right thing from now on. Remember that life's better when it's shared with friends than lived alone."

Liam gives Oliver a friendly tap on the back, then follows Aria toward the bleachers at the edge of the field.

"Looks like we did more than save Caesar in this story," Liam says.

She takes her bag and opens it. She pulls out her history book and flips to the chapter on Ancient Rome. "Oh no…"

"What?"

"It seems Caesar didn't learn his lesson."

"What do you mean?"

"He became dictator perpetuo, which means a dictator for life. He did a lot of good things, like reforming the Republic and helping the people. The Empire did not collapse under his rule but…"

"But what?"

"He was assassinated when he was just fifty-five. Sixty senators plotted against him."

"No!" Liam gasps.

"Yes. I think he was just too stubborn."

Liam gives her a sideways glance. "I hope you learned more from this story than he did."

Aria brushes off Liam's comment and adds, "He did

say no man can escape his fate before entering the Senate, which is where he got killed."

"Too bad for him. Still, I'm not going to cry. Maybe he helped the poor and did good things, but he wasn't a good man. None of them were. How can people live with so much cruelty in their hearts? I could never be like that."

Aria pauses. She's wondered the same thing herself.

"We say that, but if we'd grown up back then, it probably would have felt normal to be like them. We can't really know how we would have been or what we would have done."

Her face softens as she teases, "Especially you. You hate breaking rules. You would've followed what everyone else was doing without a second thought."

"Some rules are meant to be broken," Liam replies. "A wise girl once told me that." Then his tone changes as he says, "Aria, I need to tell you something."

"You sound serious. What is it?"

Liam checks that no one is around, then leans in and whispers, "The gods. They exist."

"What?"

"I swear. In the arena, just when I was about to get eaten, some kind of beam of light popped out of nowhere and distracted the lion. The gods saved me."

Aria stares at him for a second, then bursts out laughing, tears rolling down her cheeks.

"Liam, that was me! I stole a guard's helmet and used it to reflect sunlight into the lion's eyes!"

Liam's face falls, like his whole life has been a lie. "Seriously?"

"I *do* think magic exists, but that's not what happened here. But maybe next time, who knows?"

"Next time?" Liam shouts. "No way! Don't you *dare* drag us into another crazy, deadly trip!"

We did it! Thank you, fellow adventurers, for joining us on this adventure. Our missions wouldn't be the same without you.

Now, as you close this book and head back to your everyday lives, remember to keep that adventurous spark alive.
Let curiosity be your compass, keep exploring, and let your imaginations run wild! The world is a playground of endless wonders waiting just for you.

Stay adventurous,

Cheers!

Aria Liam

FACTS FROM THE BOOK

JULIUS CAESAR: A LIFE OF POWER

THE RISE OF JULIUS CAESAR

Julius Caesar was born in Rome around 100 BCE into a noble family, but his family was not very wealthy. As a young man, he worked hard to gain power by becoming a soldier, a speaker, and a politician. Caesar became famous as a general when he led Roman armies to victory in Gaul, which is now part of modern-day France. These victories made him very popular with soldiers and regular Roman citizens.

Bust of Julius Caesar by Andrea di Pietro di Marco Ferrucci (Italian, Fiesole 1465–1526 Florence).

At the same time, some powerful leaders in Rome grew nervous about his growing popularity. Rome was supposed to be ruled by the Senate, not by one strong man. Caesar's rising fame set the stage for major changes in Rome and big trouble for him.

CAESAR BECOMES DICTATOR

After years of fighting in Gaul, Caesar was ordered by the Senate to give up his army and return alone to Rome. The Rubicon River marked the border between Gaul and Italy, and Roman law said no general was allowed to bring an army across it. When Caesar crossed the Rubicon with his soldiers, he was openly challenging the Senate and declaring war on Rome itself. This single act started a civil war. Caesar defeated his enemies and seized control of Rome.

Caesar crossing the Rubicon. 49 Bc. Cyclopedia of Universal History, 1885. Later colouration.

Senate named Julius Caesar dictator, initially for a short period and later for life. As dictator, Caesar passed laws to help poor citizens, reduced debts, and improved the calendar (you can thank him for celebrating the New Year on January 1st, since he helped move it from March 1st). Many people admired him for making Rome stronger and more organized. Others feared he wanted to become king, which went against Roman traditions.

THE ASSASSINATION OF JULIUS CAESAR

On March 15, 44 BCE, a day known as the Ides of March, Caesar went to a meeting of the Senate. A group of senators believed killing him was the only way to save the Roman Republic. They surrounded Caesar and stabbed him many times.

According to legend, he was shocked to see his friend Brutus among the attackers. Caesar died on the floor of the Senate building.

Instead of saving the Republic, his death caused more wars and chaos. In the end, Rome became an empire ruled by emperors, not the Senate.

THE POLITICAL SYSTEM OF THE ROMAN REPUBLIC

The Roman Republic had a government designed to prevent one person from becoming too powerful. The Senate was a key part of this system and was made up of about 300 senators during much of the Republic. Senators were usually wealthy, experienced men who advised on laws, money, war, and foreign affairs, and many served for life. Even though the Senate was very influential, it did not actually pass laws.

Cesare Maccari (1840–1919), Cicero Denounces Catiline (1889), fresco, 400 x 900 cm, Palazzo Madama, Rome, Italy.

Laws were passed by assemblies of Roman citizens, where free adult men voted on new rules and leaders. Government officials, such as consuls and tribunes, presented laws to these assemblies. Each year, two consuls were elected to lead the government and the army, and they could block each other's decisions to keep power balanced. This mix of senators, elected leaders, and citizen voting helped Rome grow strong. Over time, however, this balance became harder to maintain, especially during wars and the rise of powerful figures like Julius Caesar.

ROMAN DICTATORS VS. DICTATORS TODAY

In ancient Rome, a dictator was very different from what the word usually means today. During the Roman Republic, a dictator was a legal leader chosen during emergencies like wars or major crises. Although dictators had strong powers, they were still overseen and held accountable. The Senate monitored their actions, and plebeian tribunes had the authority to veto decisions they viewed as unfair. Roman citizens could also appeal a dictator's actions, which helped protect people's rights. Dictators were given power only for a specific job and could not use it for anything else. After their term ended, they could even face trial for wrongdoing.

Today, dictators usually take power by force and rule for many years without elections. Unlike Roman dictators, modern dictators often refuse to give up control.

THE ROMAN SOCIAL LADDER

In ancient Rome, society was divided into clear levels, often called a social ladder. At the top were the patricians, wealthy families who often held power in government and the Senate. Below them were the plebeians, who made up most of the population and included farmers, workers, and soldiers. Some plebeians could become rich and important over time, especially through trade or politics.

Freedmen were formerly enslaved people who had earned or been given their freedom, but they still had fewer rights than citizens born free. At the bottom were enslaved people, who were considered property and had no legal rights. This social ladder shaped everyday life in the Roman Republic, deciding who had power, protection, and opportunity.

SLAVERY IN ANCIENT ROME

Slavery was a common and important part of life in ancient Rome. Most enslaved people were prisoners captured during wars fought by the Roman Republic. Others became enslaved because their families were very poor or because they could not pay their debts. Enslaved people worked in many places, including farms, mines,

A slavery tag (5.8 cm in diameter) inscribed with information about return. Rome, Italy, 4th century AD.
British Museum, London (UK)

homes, and even schools as teachers. Some were forced to become gladiators and fight for entertainment. Enslaved people had no freedom and were considered property, not citizens. However, some could earn or be given their freedom and become freedmen, though their lives were still difficult.

EVERYDAY LIFE IN ANCIENT ROME

FOOD IN ANCIENT ROME

Food in ancient Rome was simple for most people and depended on what they could afford. The most common meal was puls, a thick porridge made from grains like wheat or barley mixed with water. Poor families ate puls

Poor families ate puls almost every day, sometimes adding vegetables, herbs, or a little olive oil. Bread, olives, cheese, and fruit were also common foods. Wealthy Romans enjoyed larger meals with meat, fish, eggs, and fancy sauces. What you ate in Rome clearly showed how rich or poor you were.

A Roman House

Homes in ancient Rome depended on how rich a family was. Wealthy Romans lived in a house called a domus, which was built around an open courtyard called an atrium. The atrium let in light and rainwater, which was collected in a small pool. Rooms opened onto the courtyard, and there was often a garden at the back of the house. Poorer people lived in apartment buildings called insulae, which could be crowded and unsafe.

Ideal reconstruction of an atrium by German architect Strack Johann Heinrich (1805-1880).

Religion in Ancient Rome

Religion was an important part of daily life in ancient Rome, not just something practiced on special days. Romans believed in many gods and goddesses who controlled different parts of life, such as Jupiter, the king of the gods, Juno (the goddess of marriage and family), and Minerva (the goddess of wisdom, learning, and crafts).

Capitoline Triad, Jupiter, Juno and Minerva seated on the throne, from Trier. Roman civilisation, 2nd century. Museo Della Civiltà Romana, Rome (Italy)

People believed the gods protected the Roman Republic if they were honored properly. Families worshipped at home using small shrines called lararia, where they prayed to household spirits.

Public ceremonies, sacrifices, and festivals were held to please the gods. One important festival was Quinquatria, which was celebrated in late March in honor of Minerva.

Money

Romans used coins made of bronze, silver, and gold to buy what they needed. The most common silver coin was called the denarius. Soldiers, workers, and merchants were often paid in denarii for their work.

Fashion

Clothing was very important because it showed a person's social rank. Most men wore simple tunics, while important male citizens wore togas during public events. Women wore long dresses called stolas, often with shawls.

Colors mattered too—blue was disliked because Romans connected it with barbarians and sadness, so it was rarely worn. Clean and simple clothing was seen as a sign of good morals and self-control.

Hobbies

Romans enjoyed many hobbies and ways to relax, but not all of them were approved by the law. Gambling was officially illegal because Roman leaders believed it was immoral and could lead to bad behavior. Laws were passed to stop people from gambling, and officials tried to enforce them. However, gambling was still very popular, and many Romans played dice games in secret or pretended they were playing "for fun."

Children played board games and games of skill like ludus latrunculorum, a strategy game similar to checkers or chess, and tabula, a game played with pieces and dice on a board. These games helped children practice thinking, counting, and planning.

Romans also enjoyed watching plays, athletic events, and shows in amphitheaters.

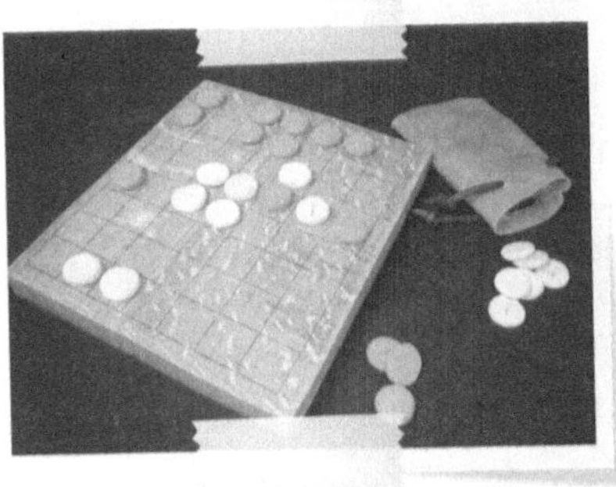

The game Ludus Latrunculorum, Academy of Historical Arts (UK)

Disease in Ancient Rome

Disease was a serious danger for people living in ancient Rome. While plagues did appear at times, the biggest killers were infectious diseases such as malaria, tuberculosis, typhoid fever, and stomach illnesses like gastroenteritis. The most dangerous malaria was a severe type that spread in warm weather and often became deadly in late summer and autumn. From July to October, about 30,000 people were estimated to die each year, and Roman writers even warned people to leave the city during these "sickly" months.

Death rates were lower from November to February, though elderly people were still at risk during winter. Women and young children, especially ages one to five, were the most vulnerable. Crowded housing, poor hygiene, weak diets, and many new arrivals to the city made it easy for diseases to spread and hard to survive them.

The Place of Women and Men in Society

Men and women had very different roles in Roman life, especially during the time of the Roman Republic. Men worked outside the home, served in the army, and could vote or hold political office. Women managed households, raised children, and could own property, but they were not allowed to vote or rule. Education depended on wealth: rich families sent children to school to learn reading, writing, math, and public speaking. Poor children usually learned trades by working with their families instead. These rules and routines shaped daily life for everyone in ancient Rome.

Ancient Roman street scene, J. Williamson.

The City of Rome

Rome was the capital of the Roman empire and one of the largest cities of the ancient world. Many buildings and symbols showed how proud Romans were of their government. One famous symbol was SPQR, which stood for Senatus Populusque Romanus, meaning "The Senate and the People of Rome." This phrase showed that Rome believed it was ruled together by its leaders and its citizens, and it appeared on buildings, banners, and coins.

Detail from the mosaic floor in the Gallery Vittorio Emanuele II in Milan
Detail from the mosaic floor in the Gallery Vittorio Emanuele II in Rome.
Picture by Giovanni Dall'Orto, June 22 2007.

At the center of the city, the Curia was the Senate building where Roman senators met to debate laws and make decisions for the Roman Republic. Nearby was the Forum, where people shopped, listened to speeches, and met friends.

Rendering of the Roman Forum as it may have appeared during the Late Empire. By A derivative work of a 3D model by Lasha Tskhondia .

The Tiber River flowed through Rome and was used to bring food, goods, and travelers into the city. High above the city stood Capitoline Hill, one of Rome's most sacred places. At the top was a temple dedicated to Jupiter, Juno, and Minerva, the most important Roman gods who were believed to protect Rome.

Romans also cared a great deal about cleanliness and public life. Public baths were large buildings where people came not only to wash but also to exercise, relax, and socialize. Baths had warm, hot, and cold rooms, and most Romans visited them often. Toilets, called latrines, were public and shared by many people at once. They had long stone seats with holes and used flowing water to carry waste away. Instead of toilet paper, Romans used a shared sponge on a stick, which was cleaned between uses. These places show how Romans mixed daily needs with community life.

A reconstruction drawing of the interior of a Roman latrines by artist Philip Corke.

The Colosseum

The Colosseum is one of the most famous buildings from ancient Rome, but it did not exist during Julius Caesar's lifetime. In this book, it appears during Caesar's time for storytelling reasons, but in reality, it was built later, starting around 72 CE and opening in 80 CE.

During Caesar's lifetime, games took place in earlier amphitheaters as well as in open spaces like the Forum. The Colosseum later became the largest and most famous place for these spectacles.

The Colosseum was designed to impress and to manage huge crowds safely. It was an enormous oval structure made from stone and concrete, with more than 80 entrances that allowed tens of thousands of spectators to enter and leave quickly. Inside, seats were carefully arranged by social class, placing senators close to the action and poorer citizens higher up. Beneath the arena floor was a hidden underground system of tunnels, cages, and elevators used to move animals, scenery, and gladiators into the arena. One exit was called the "Gate of Death," where the bodies of fighters who did not survive were carried out.

3D model of the Colosseum by Squir.

Gladiators and Roman Entertainment

The main attraction in Roman arenas was gladiator fights, including battles between gladiators and wild animals. Gladiators were usually enslaved people, prisoners of war, or criminals, though some free men volunteered for fame or money. They trained in special schools and learned how to fight with different weapons and armor. Some events, called venationes, featured fighters facing lions, bears, or other exotic animals brought from across the empire.

In early Roman history, gladiators were more likely to die in the arena. As the games became more organized and gladiators more expensive to train, owners did not want them killed unless necessary. By the later periods, many fights ended when one fighter surrendered or was spared by the crowd or officials. Romans enjoyed many kinds of entertainment, not just gladiator fights. Chariot races were extremely popular and took place in large stadiums like the Circus Maximus. Some shows even included naumachiae, or mock sea battles, where ships fought in flooded arenas.

Color lithograph depicting gladiators in a Roman arena by French painter Jean-Léon Gérôme (1824–1904)

Spartacus: The Gladiator Who Fought Back

One of the most famous gladiators in Roman history was Spartacus. Spartacus was a Thracian, a warrior from a region north of Greece, known for its strong fighters. He had once served as a soldier but was later captured by the Romans.

After his capture, he was enslaved and sent to a gladiator school in southern Italy. In 73 BCE, Spartacus escaped with other gladiators and led a massive slave rebellion against Rome. Thousands of enslaved people joined him as they marched across Italy. Although he was eventually defeated and killed, Spartacus became a lasting symbol of courage and the fight for freedom in ancient Rome.

The Roman Vigiles

In ancient Rome, there was no police force like we have today, but there was a group called the Vigiles. The Vigiles were city workers whose job was to help keep Rome safe. There were about 7,000 Vigiles in total, spread across the city. They dealt with criminals such as thieves and helped capture enslaved people who had run away. The Vigiles also acted as Rome's fire brigade, which was very important because fires spread quickly in crowded neighborhoods. They worked day and night to protect the people living in the capital of the Roman Republic.

ABOUT THE AUTHOR

Coline Monsarrat grew up believing books were gateways to magical realms where anything was possible. Her love for history and her endless curiosity shaped her belief that life is an adventure waiting to be written and we are the authors of our own stories.

Inspired by the wonders of the past, Coline created the *Aria & Liam* series to spark young readers' imaginations and take them into the wonders of history.

A citizen of the world, she has lived on four continents and who knows where her next chapter will unfold?

www.colinemonsarrat.com

instagram.com/colinemonsarrat

MEET THE TEAM

Editing and proofreading: Two Birds Author Services

And once again, Andrea and Michele made this story better. Thank you to the two most fabulous editors a writer could ask for.

http://twobirdsauthorservices.com/

Cover and illustrations: Draftss

Illustrators: Ragini Ingle and Harsh Chaudhary

Design Manager : Kaustavi Baruah

Project Manager : Vanshika Goyal

A huge thank you to Harsh, Ragini, Kaustavi, and Vanshika at Draftss for bringing the characters to life. I'm so grateful for your incredible work.

https://draftss.com/

Inside book layout: Jessica Miller

Vector files and images: Freepik and Getty images